PURRFECT MESS

THE MYSTERIES OF MAX 50

NIC SAINT

PURRFECT MESS

The Mysteries of Max 50

Copyright © 2021 by Nic Saint

Edited by Chereese Graves

www.nicsaint.com

Give feedback on the book at: info@nicsaint.com

facebook.com/nicsaintauthor
@nicsaintauthor

First Edition

Printed in the U.S.A

PURRFECT MESS

Meet the Boggles

It was supposed to be a quiet time, a time of happiness and familial bliss. Odelia was on maternity leave, and so a pleasant vacation was to be had by all. Unfortunately the fates decided differently. First a Prime Minister drifted in, expelled from England, where he'd run into a spot of bother, and soon our home was no longer that beacon of tranquility and quiet joy.

In his wake, more visitors popped over, turning the house into a glorified Airbnb and Odelia into a reluctant hostess. And then when Gran decided to start a wellness resort in her backyard, we finally decided enough was enough and were on the verge of migrating to more welcoming shores. But of course we didn't. Instead, we stuck it out, deciding that our humans needed us now more than ever.

CHAPTER 1

"Max?"

"Mh?"

"Do you think James Bond could be played by a cat?"

It was one of those questions that makes you think, and so think is what I did. "What brought this on?" I said in an attempt at prevarication.

"Chase said that they're looking for a new actor to play James Bond, since the previous one feels he's too old for the role, and Odelia said they might pick a woman this time. So I was wondering why not a cat, you know?"

"I like your thinking, Dooley," I said. "Why not a cat indeed?"

"I mean, the time that only middle-aged white males could play James Bond is well and truly behind us. And to appeal to a larger demographic they should consider their options. And everybody likes cats, so they've got that pre-existing audience."

"I couldn't agree more," I said. We'd only recently watched a James Bond movie on television, all of us cozily ensconced in the living room, the humans riveted to their TV set, and us cats wondering what all the fuss was about as usual. "Though it might be hard to find a cat that fits the part," I said, my thought processes a little sluggish on this, a lazy Saturday morning in the Kingsley home.

Dooley and I were in the backyard, enjoying those first few rays that do so much to warm up one's bones, the dewy grass nice and cool against my belly. Our humans—Odelia and Chase—were still in bed, and so was baby Grace, the latest addition to the clan.

"Brutus could do it," said Dooley. "He'd be perfect for the role."

"You're forgetting one thing, my friend," I said. "James Bond has a license to kill, and to do that he needs to be able to handle a gun, and since cats aren't naturally equipped by an otherwise wise and benevolent creator to handle a firearm, I think Brutus would be dropped from the lineup at his first audition. In fact he probably wouldn't even make it past the first selection."

This was enough to give my best friend pause. At least for a few minutes. But then he rallied. "Maybe they can adopt a strict no-gun policy? Brutus could use his claws when he's under attack. I'll bet he can be equally lethal—or even more so—with his claws than by using a gun. He could be the new gun-less Bond."

"True, true," I admitted. Though frankly I had a feeling the James Bond aficionados might not agree if after sixty years the famous franchise suddenly went firearm-free. Then again, the question was probably moot, since as far as I knew, Brutus had never expressed an interest in being the next Bond.

"I bet they'll cast a dog," Dooley said moodily. "They always do."

"A dog would make a great spy," I said, trying to cheer

him up. "Dogs are very photogenic. And popular, too. I'll bet if the next Bond was a dog it would be a big hit."

"Who would be a hit?" suddenly asked a voice in my rear.

It was, of course, our friend Harriet. She and her boyfriend Brutus now came sashaying in our direction, straight from the rose bushes where they like to spend some quality time of a morning—or an afternoon or even a night.

"The new James Bond," said Dooley without looking up. "They're casting a dog."

"A dog!" said Brutus. "You're not serious."

"Dooley is simply speculating," I hastened to say.

"Isn't that just typical?" Harriet scoffed. "It's always the same pets who have all the luck. I'm telling you, it's a dog's world out there, and us cats are always picked last."

"Dooley was just saying how you'd make the perfect Bond," I said, trying to interject a modicum of optimism and cheerfulness into the conversation.

"I know," said Harriet, simpering a little.

"No, I actually meant Bru—"

"I'd make some changes, of course," she blithely went on. "For one thing I'd make sure they drop that dreadfully dreary color scheme." She sighed excitedly. "I'm seeing lots of pinks and yellows. Maybe even some powder blue. And of course only happy faces from now on. Happy happy happy. And maybe we could do a big dance number to open the movie, with lots and lots of showcats, like in *La La Land*." She gave her partner a coy look. "My name is Bond. Harriet Bond."

"Excellent," Brutus murmured, though I could tell he wasn't as happy as he could have been at this example of creative casting. And you have to admit: Brutus Bond does have a nice ring to it. Better than Max Bond at any rate. Or even Dooley Bond.

Then again, it was no use speculating, since no Bond

3

producer in their right mind would ever cast a cat in the coveted role of Ian Fleming's famous secret agent. Cats are simply too cute. And a cute Bond is a big no-no. And so instead of thinking of ways and means of saving the planet from a dastardly evil genius and his henchmen, Harriet joined us on the lawn, and let the sunlight play about her noble visage.

Brutus, meanwhile, ventured into the house to subject his food bowl to a spot check, and as the birds tweeted in a nearby tree, and a neighbor took his lawnmower for a test run, I soon found myself drifting off to sleep. And I probably would have dreamt of Bond girls and fancy cars and nifty spy gadgetry if not suddenly a fire engine started screaming nearby.

We were wide awake within milliseconds, and it took me a while to realize it wasn't a fire that was about to consume some innocent home, but baby Grace who had decided that she required nourishment and she required it right now!

"Oh, dear," said Harriet, once she had her heartbeat under control again. "I don't think I'll ever get used to that terrible sound."

I could have told her that if she was going to be the next James Bond, there probably were worse things she needed to tackle than the sound of a hungry infant, but I wisely kept my tongue.

We all directed a curious look at the upstairs window, behind which I could easily picture the homely scene that was now playing out: Chase and Odelia would have immediately woken up, and were presumably staggering, still sleep drunk, in the direction of the cradle that housed the source of all this clamor. Moments later, the screaming stopped, and we all shared a look of satisfaction. Odelia had done it again: she'd managed to tame the savage beast that lurks behind the pure face of innocence.

"Who knew that such a tiny human could produce such a big sound?" said Harriet, shaking her head in wonder.

"She'll have a great career as an opera singer," said Dooley. "She already has the volume, now all she has to do is work on expanding her repertoire."

He was right. So far Grace's performances kept within the one-note range.

From next door, Fifi came trotting up. Fifi is a Yorkshire Terrier, and probably one of the nicest dogs alive—and I don't say this lightly, as everyone knows that most dogs are foul creatures who like nothing better than to chase cats up trees.

"Kurt isn't happy, you guys," she said as she joined us.

"Kurt is never happy," I said. Kurt is Fifi's human, and our perpetually grumpy next-door neighbor. Though what he isn't happy about tends to vary day by day.

"What isn't he happy about this time?" asked Brutus, popping out through the pet flap, satisfied that his bowl still contained the necessary foodstuffs.

"It's the baby," said Fifi. "He says she's way too loud, and if this keeps up he's going to file a noise complaint."

"Good luck with that," said Brutus. "Doesn't he know Grace's dad is a cop?"

"Oh, he knows, which is why he won't file the complaint in Hampton Cove. He's going straight to the top."

"The top?" I asked, intrigued. "You mean the Mayor?"

"The Governor," said Fifi. "He's going to claim that his rights as a citizen and a taxpayer are being trampled on. And he says there's a precedent."

"What precedent?"

"Remember how they wanted to build an airport in Happy Bays last year and how the neighbors successfully petitioned against it? Well, he says the same principle applies."

I have to confess we were all a little flabbergasted, but finally I pointed out, "A baby isn't an airplane, Fifi."

"Max is absolutely right," Dooley chimed in. "For one thing, babies don't fly." He turned to me. "Do they?"

"No, Dooley," I said. "Babies don't fly."

"Unlike the storks that deliver them," said Dooley with a nod in my direction.

"I know that," said Fifi, "and Kurt knows that, but he says she makes the same noise as a jumbo jet, and since he was here first, that dreadful baby has to go. And if the Governor doesn't get rid of her, he's taking his case up to the President."

"Dreadful baby?" said Harriet. "Did he really call Grace a dreadful baby?"

"Actually he used a much stronger term," said Fifi with a touch of bashfulness. "But I don't want to be rude."

"Kurt isn't a very nice person," said Dooley.

"He's nice to me," said Fifi. "But you're right. He's not very nice to other people."

"And babies," said Dooley.

"Babies are people, too, Dooley," said Harriet. "Only they're a lot smaller."

"They're like miniature people," Brutus explained with an indulgent smile. "They have tiny toes and tiny fingers and tiny ears and a tiny nose and—"

"Yes, yes, we get the picture," I interrupted my friend's vivid word picture of what, exactly, constitutes a human baby.

"They're not really going to get rid of Grace, are they, Max?" said Dooley, a look of concern now marring my friend's funny little face.

"Of course not," I said. "The whole idea is ridiculous."

Still, I have to admit I wasn't sanguine about Fifi's report, straight from the front lines. Kurt has been known to throw the odd shoe in our direction, you see, expressing in word and gesture his displeasure with our vocal performance of an evening. Was it so hard to imagine the lengths he'd go to to rid himself of an admittedly vociferous infant? After all, no man is born a shoe thrower. As a young boy Kurt probably threw matches at passing cats, then gradually worked his way up to twigs and sticks, then shoes, and now he was moving into the baby removal business. If he kept this up, pretty soon he'd morph into a full-fledged Bond villain and construct a secret lair underneath his lawn so he could destroy the world.

CHAPTER 2

*V*esta Muffin hadn't slept well. Now she'd read in some magazine that once you reach a certain age you need less shut-eye but lately she'd been more awake than asleep during those restless nights. It had become so bad she'd developed a habit of getting up in the middle of the night and going for a midnight walk around the block. The fresh air and the brisk exercise usually tired her out to such an extent that by the time she tumbled into bed again, she slept like the proverbial baby… until what seemed like moments later it was time to start her day.

She'd talked to Tex, her son-in-law, who was a doctor and was supposed to know about this stuff, but he'd merely offered her some platitudes about old age that she hadn't appreciated in the least.

"Old age, my foot," she now muttered as she threw off the comforter and swung her feet to the floor. Once again she felt she hadn't enjoyed nearly enough sleep, and feared that if this kept up, she might even develop issues with her ticker. Hadn't she read somewhere that insomnia could lead to heart problems?

"Chamomile tea," her daughter Marge had advised. "And no screens before bedtime."

"I hate tea, and I never had trouble falling asleep after watching TV before."

"I'm not talking about TV, Ma. I'm talking about your phone."

"My phone? What's wrong with my phone?"

"Blue light," Marge had said, rather mysteriously, she thought.

"Blue light, my ass," she said as she threw her curtains wide to see what the weather was like. The sun was benevolently splashing its rays across a grateful world, but Vesta squinted, giving it the evil eye. "Sunlight, that's the problem," she said. Maybe she had to move up North, where they never had any light, blue or otherwise. Wasn't there some place in Alaska where they never got any light at all? Months and months of utter and complete darkness? Now that would probably lull her to sleep—a nice long winter sleep. Like a bear. Or a hedgehog. Then again, since she hated the cold, that probably wasn't an option either.

She sighed deeply and shuffled out of her room and into the bathroom, which, lucky for her, hadn't yet been occupied by the rest of the household. With a flick of the wrist, she locked the door, and started the tedious daily ritual of addressing her personal hygiene needs—which were plenty and getting greater every day.

❧

*T*ex awoke with a start, lifting his head half an inch from the pillow then letting it fall back again with a groan of dismay. It was his fervent wish that one morning he'd be able to get up before his mother-in-law, so he could be the first one to occupy the bathroom, but so far he hadn't yet succeeded in fulfilling this modest desire.

"We should have built a second bathroom," he now told his wife, who was stirring next to him.

"We still could," she muttered, her eyes firmly closed.

"But where? There's no space for a second bathroom."

"We could build one in the garden house," Marge suggested.

He gave this some thought. It was an idea, of course. When they'd recently rebuilt the house, he'd suggested to the architect to squeeze in a second bathroom, but the man had convinced them it wasn't feasible, nor was it necessary, since they were only three occupants. He'd pointed out that the man had never lived under the same roof as his mother-in-law, and the architect had given him a look of such compassion he'd been moved to tears and had never mentioned the topic again.

"We'll never get permission," he said as he rubbed the sleep from his eyes.

"We could build it illegally," said Marge.

He directed an indulgent smile at his wife of twenty-five years. "We're talking major plumbing, honey. No plumber would touch the project without the necessary permits."

Marge yawned and stretched, then gave him a yearning look. "For once in my life I want to be the first to get into the bathroom, Tex. The first one to take a shower."

"I know," he said. "Me, too." He sighed a wistful sigh. "But as I get older I'm starting to realize it's simply not in the cards for us. One of those pipe dreams like winning the lottery or finishing the crossword puzzle. We've been getting up earlier and earlier and she's still beating us to it. The woman never sleeps."

"And spends what seems like hours in there."

"Worse than Odelia when she was a teenager."

For a moment they both were silent as they contemplated ways and means of fixing a problem that had been vexing them since they'd invited Marge's mom to share their home with them. "We could always hire one of those cowboy builders," Marge suggested.

"You mean like the ones that destroyed our old home? Aren't they in jail?"

"There must be others," said Marge with a touch of desperation. "Others like them?"

He swallowed away a lump of unease. It was one thing to dream of going down a certain route, but quite another to actually go ahead and venture into illegality. Theirs had been a life built on a strict adherence to the rule of law. He never even jaywalked, and always dropped his litter in the appropriate receptacle. So the prospect of suddenly venturing into a life of crime gave him quite a jolt.

He blinked. "Are you sure about this?" he asked, his voice a little hoarse as he nervously licked his lips.

The voice of Marge's mother suddenly rang out. She'd burst into song and was obviously taking one of those long, hot showers she loved so much, using up all the hot water and leaving nothing for the rest of the family. *"I'm a poor, lonesome cowboy!"* she was belting at the top of her voice. *"And I'm a long way from home!"*

Marge hesitated but for a moment, then nodded eagerly. "Let's do it," she whispered.

In spite of his misgivings, he whispered back, "Don't tell your mother?"

Marge mimicked locking her lips and throwing away the key. "Cross my heart."

"And hope to die," he murmured. "Though on second thought, maybe scratch that."

"Let's break the law, Clyde," Marge smiled.

"Let's build ourselves an illegal bathroom, Bonnie," he smiled back.

And so it was decided. After walking the straight and narrow for forty-eight years—well, maybe forty-seven, since the first year of their lives they admittedly hadn't done a lot of walking—Tex and Marge Poole were embracing the life of crime—and the pitfalls of DIY plumbing.

CHAPTER 3

G race had been washed and fed and was sleeping peacefully in her crib, and so Odelia sighed with relief as she nursed her cup of tea and took a breather at the kitchen counter. Chase had left for work and the house was suddenly very quiet, which was exactly the way she liked it. The cats were outside, escaping the din and hubbub a newborn baby inevitably brings, and since she was on maternity leave from work, frankly she had nothing to do and nothing to occupy her time but to take care of Grace.

She idly flipped through a few of the updates her boss had posted on the *Gazette* website and found herself reading some of the articles her replacement had written with a critical eye. Then, realizing how silly she was being, she put down the phone and suddenly found herself wondering what she would do for the rest of the day.

Having spent all of her adult life occupied in gainful employment, this sudden lull in what otherwise was a modestly stellar career was a little disconcerting to say the least. Dan had told her to take it easy for a while, and not to spend even one second thinking about the job. And Chase had told her that from now on she wasn't to even contemplate assisting him in his own job—no running around fighting crime with a baby tucked in her arms!—and even her uncle had said that her days of gleefully hobnobbing with notorious killers and other scum of the Hampton Cove underworld were finally over—and not a moment too soon!

But if she wasn't a reporter, and she wasn't a detective, then what was she?

Grace made a slight gurgling sound in her sleep and Odelia smiled. First and foremost, of course, she was a mother, and maybe that was enough. At least for now.

She did wonder how her cats felt about this whole transition to a more peaceful and uneventful life. Max had assisted her and Chase so many times in collaring criminals and identifying villains that he must be experiencing withdrawal symptoms. Though to be honest he seemed perfectly happy with this new phase in their lives. Content, even.

Just then, her phone vibrated and she immediately picked up, darting a quick glance to Grace. She lowered her voice, not wanting to wake up the baby and said, "Yes, Odelia Kingsley speaking?"

It was an unknown number, and even though she probably should adopt Gran's stance on unknown callers: namely, to ignore them and when they don't leave a message report them to your provider and then block them, she simply couldn't. On your true reporter, worth their salt, a call from an unknown number acts very much like the proverbial red flag to a bull: it heats up the blood and makes their nerve endings sizzle with anticipatory excitement. For who knows, it could be the President, offering an exclusive sit-down to discuss their latest brainwave. Or Adele, suggesting a duet for her next album '35,' or Kim Kardashian, offering a part in her new reality show. Or it could even be a publisher suggesting they publish her autobiography. A girl can only dream!

"Hey, Odelia," the voice on the other end spoke. "It's Tessa. Is this a bad time?"

She gulped a little, then managed, "Oh, hey, Tessa!"

She'd met Tessa Torrance and her husband Prince Dante in England a while back, when the couple had been relentlessly hounded by the tabloids and eventually driven out of the country by those rabid newshounds.

"I'm sorry to drop this on you," said Tessa, "but I'm afraid I need a favor. Again."

"Absolutely," she said immediately. "Anything."

"The thing is... a dear, dear friend of ours finds himself in something of a pickle. And so I was wondering if you could help him out. I wouldn't be asking you this," she hastened to add, "if it wasn't extremely important. You see, he urgently needs a place to lie low for a while, a place where no one would think to look for him. In other words: Hampton Cove."

"Of course," she said, blinking a few times at this unexpected request. Then she produced what she hoped was a sufficiently airy chuckle. "He's not a fugitive from justice, is he? Cause I'm not sure Chase would approve if we were harboring a known criminal."

For a moment Tessa didn't speak, and Odelia's cheeks colored. Then her friend said, "I'm afraid you're going to have to trust me on this, Odelia."

So this man *was* a criminal! Oh, dear.

"So can I tell him to head to your place?"

"Um..."

"I would host him myself but you know how I'm constantly under surveillance by some of the same paps that drove us out of England. Can you believe they're using drones now, trying to snap a shot of us walking in our own backyard?"

She murmured a sound of commiseration, even as she wondered how she was going to explain to Chase that she had agreed to supply room and board to some British crook.

"He hasn't… *murdered* anyone, has he?" she finally insisted.

This time it was Tessa's turn to produce a light chuckle. "No, Odelia. He's not a murderer. But he is in big trouble, and I can't thank you and Chase enough for doing this."

"So—"

"Okay, I gotta go. Dante is calling me. Toodle-pip, honey. And thanks again."

"But I—" But the Duchess of Essex was gone and she found herself staring at her phone in mild horror. Chase was going to be very unhappy when he discovered what she'd let herself in for this time. At least the man—whoever he was—hadn't murdered anyone, which was a small consolation.

She chewed her bottom lip as she wondered where they were going to put this mystery guest. They'd turned the guest room into a nursery, so that was out of the question. And she couldn't very well ask Tessa's friend to sleep on the couch. And so it was with a groan of dismay that she finally picked up her phone again.

"Mom?" she said as the call connected. "Help!"

CHAPTER 4

⌘

"*I* have to say that I like this new life of ours," I said. I'd been lying on my back for a while, which is one of my favorite positions when in repose, and gazing up at a blue sky that was both majestic and a little bit scary, since it was filled with birds. And as everyone knows, some species of birds can be pretty keen on snapping up any bit of nourishment their beady eye can see, and they're especially keen on a juicy morsel like me.

"What new life?" asked Dooley, who was also taking in some sun on the belly.

"Well, this new life we're living. With the baby and all?"

Dooley turned his head to face me, and I could tell that he was not a little bit puzzled. "I don't understand, Max. What new life with the baby?"

And then I remembered that I hadn't yet related the conversation Odelia and Chase had been having the night before. About the future and all of that stuff.

"Okay, so Odelia has been working like a beaver fighting crime, right?" I said.

"Uh-huh."

17

"Catching criminals and putting the bad guys behind bars?"

"Okay."

"But now she has the baby, and so that part of her life is over."

He chewed on this for a moment, then came back with: "I don't understand."

"Okay, look. So when you want to catch a criminal, you automatically put yourself in danger."

"Uh-huh."

"But now that she has the baby, she can't do that kind of thing anymore. Imagine if she gets hurt? What's going to happen to Grace?"

"She'll be sad?"

I wasn't fully convinced that babies are capable of feeling sad at the unexpected demise of one or both of their parental units, but that wasn't the point I was trying to make. "Sure she'll be sad," I said, "but more importantly: who's going to take care of her when Odelia is gone?"

Dooley's eyes went wide. "Odelia is gone?!" he cried. "Where did she go?!"

"I'm just describing a hypothetical situation, Dooley," I said. "The kind of situation a writer would describe as a 'what if' situation. What if Odelia keeps putting herself in jeopardy? What if something happens to her?"

He mulled this over for a moment, then said, "I'd be very sad if that happens."

"I think we'd all be very sad if that happens, and so Chase and Uncle Alec have put their foot down: no more police business for us. Which means no more criminal investigations and no more getting involved in the sordid side of society."

"So we're done being cat sleuths?"

"We're done being cat sleuths."

His face lit up. "I think that's great."

"Do you? Do you really?"

"Of course! These are some very dangerous people we've been chasing all this time, Max. And just being close to them we could have ended up corollary damage."

"I think you mean collateral damage."

"So we're officially retired now?"

"We're officially retired," I confirmed.

"Nice."

I closed my eyes for a moment, seeing as there were no big birds on the horizon that I could see. No vultures or pterodactyls or suchlike.

"But we're still going to spy out information for Odelia, aren't we?" Dooley interrupted my peaceful slumber.

"I don't think so, buddy. Odelia is officially retired, too."

"But she's still a reporter, right?"

I shook my head. "Odelia is a mother now, and she has Grace to take care of. So she won't be working for the paper anymore." Or at least that's what I'd heard from listening in on her conversations with her husband. Even Chase wasn't going to be risking life and limb so much anymore, as Uncle Alec had hired a new detective to take over part of his workload—some eager whippersnapper who was going to tackle crime with distinct fervor. Chase had been promoted and was going to take on a more senior role at the precinct, giving colleagues the benefit of his extensive experience.

"But… if Odelia isn't a detective anymore, and she's not a reporter anymore, then what is she going to do from now on?" he asked, a slight sense of panic clear in his voice. "I mean, what are *we* going to do, Max?" I glanced in his direction and could see that his features were contorted in abject confusion. "Who are we when we're not cat sleuths?!!!"

A cat psychologist, had one been present, would have immediately recognized the symptoms as a clear indication of an impending crisis of identity. And as Dooley's words penetrated my admittedly thick skull, suddenly I found myself sharing his vivid concern.

When we weren't cat sleuths anymore, or spies for Odelia —what were we?!!!

&

*F*ifi, who'd also been enjoying the way today was turning out to be one of those gloriously sunny days when the sun really gives of its best, couldn't help but overhear the musings of her two best friends Max and Dooley. She might have been sunbathing on her side of the hedge—Kurt got a little anxious each time he lost sight of her —but since Max and Dooley were only a few yards away, and hedges aren't soundproof, she had heard their conversation word for word.

And it had got her thinking. She'd always admired Max as being one of those brainy cats—cats that can solve any riddle big or small. In the time they'd been friends and neighbors, she'd known the big blorange cat to catch many a criminal by working his way through clues that were too difficult for her to fathom, and it had only served to make her admiration for her neighbor increase with leaps and bounds.

And so now that Max's stellar career had abruptly come to an end, she felt sorry for the cat. Dooley was right, of course: if they weren't cat sleuths anymore, then what were they? Too young to retire, but perhaps not too old to change careers? It was a difficult puzzle to figure out for a tiny Yorkie whose brain hadn't been constructed along the lines of her brainy feline neighbor. It just made her wonder what the future would bring. She hoped it was sunshine and rainbows.

CHAPTER 5

*T*ex was subjecting his garden house to a closer inspection. It wasn't a very large garden house, as garden houses go, but in his estimation it was certainly big enough to house a bathroom of modest proportions. In his infinite wisdom he had decided that he wasn't going to engage a cowboy builder after all. He was going to do the work himself. How hard could it be? Also, it was a lot cheaper that way, and the less people were involved in the erection of this illegal construction, the better. Marge had given him her blessing, and had suggested he ask his son-in-law for a helping hand and also her brother Alec. Together, the three of them would build a bijou bathroom—he was absolutely sure about it.

And so it was with a grin of anticipatory satisfaction that he stepped into the garden house, measuring tape in hand, and started measuring. He measured the floor, he measured the ceiling, he measured the windows—he even measured the lawnmower. And he was still busy measuring for all he was worth when an irascible voice brought him out of his measuring mesmerization.

"You're not seriously considering building a bathroom out here, are you?" the voice demanded.

He didn't even have to look up to identify the owner of the voice. It was, of course, his mother-in-law. "And what if I am?" he asked, injecting a modicum of rebellion into his tone. He wondered how she'd found out. Then again, Vesta had a way of sniffing out secrets. She wasn't the head of the neighborhood watch by accident. He turned to face what he often described as the bane of his existence.

"Why, it's way too small in here," said Vesta, subjecting the dusty interior to a critical frown. "If you're going to build something, you gotta think big, Tex—a lot bigger than this."

"What are you talking about?" he said coldly.

"Look, you're going to spend a lot of time and a lot of money on this thing, so why not scale up? Create something we can all enjoy: you, me, Marge, Odelia—the whole family."

He didn't want to point out the obvious: that the only reason he was building this second bathroom was because Vesta spent a disproportionate amount of time in the first one. But he still felt it incumbent upon him to make matters clear from the start. "Make no mistake, Vesta," he said. "This bathroom is going to be ours—mine and Marge's." He tapped his chest to add emphasis to his words, in case his monster-in-law missed the point. "That bathroom?" he said, pointing in the general direction of the house, "will be your bathroom. And this one? Mine."

"Sure, sure," said Vesta as she fingered her pointy chin. "So just hear me out, will ya? What if you tore this thing down—it's an eyesore and who needs a lawnmower anyway?" He was going to point out that the grass didn't mow itself, but she went on, "And then you buy one of those ready-made saunas and install the whole thing right here." She stepped back and pointed to the fence that separated the Poole family's little corner of the world from the field that stretched out behind them. "If I were you I'd get rid of that fence as well. I'm thinking jacuzzi, sauna, maybe even a pool —so what do you say?"

She was standing, hands akimbo, glancing up at him with the kind of fire in her eyes he didn't like to see. "We can't tear down that fence," was all he could think of to say.

"And why not? Who's gonna notice?"

"Blake Carrington, that's who." Blake owned that field, and built that fence.

She made a throwaway gesture with her hand. "Blake doesn't care if you expand your property a little. Heck, he might even like it. At least something useful will be done with the land. And if he kicks up a fuss, you simply give him a free year-round pass to use our spa and sauna complex. Trust me—he'll love it."

"Spa and sauna complex!" Tex cried, horrified.

"Sure." A dreamy look had stolen over the crusty old dame's face. "I can see it now: the Poole Spa & Pool. Got a nice ring to it, don't you think? I'll bet you could charge twenty bucks just for the privilege of getting access to the place, and you could even sell season tickets—or don't they do that kind of stuff with spas?"

Tex's hands had flown to his head, and his fingers were digging into his white hair of their own accord—and his hair was white for a reason! "Season tickets!"

"Before you know it this will be the hottest show in town, bud—mark my words."

"No," he said. "No way."

"And I'll tell you something else. My friend Scarlett's great-nephew Kevin is something of a computer wizard. And if you ask him nicely he'll whip you up a great little website. Free publicity. People will be flocking to our spa from all over town. Heck, from all over the county! The Poole Spa & Pool will be the place to be!"

"Absolutely out of the question. This is my bathroom. Mine and mine alone."

"Oh, don't be such a miser, Tex," said Vesta, prodding him in the small of the back with a bony finger. "Live a little." And with these words, she strode off, leaving Tex feeling as if he'd just been in a close encounter with a wrecking ball. The sensation was not unfamiliar. Vesta often had that effect on him.

The sound of someone gently scraping his throat reached his ear, and when he whirled around, he found himself face to face with Ted, his next-door neighbor.

"Building yourself a spa, huh, Tex?" said Ted. "Nice."

"I'm not building a spa," he said emphatically.

"Poole Spa & Pool? Gotta admit it's got a nice ring to it."

"There's not going to be a Poole Spa & Pool."

"Well, I hope that when it's finished you'll give your favorite neighbors a free pass. I love me a nice sauna and so does the wife."

"There won't be a sauna," he said through gritted teeth.

Ted's smile lost something of its avuncularity. "I hope you got all your papers in order. Cause if you don't, I'd hate to be the one to tell the council one of our neighbors has gone and built himself an illegal structure in his backyard. They don't take kindly to that kind of thing, you know. I'm talking fines, Tex. Big fines."

Tex freely ground his teeth for a few moments. "It's just a bathroom, Ted."

"So you say."

"Just a small, tiny bathroom."

"I hear you, buddy. And if you give me and the wife a free pass to your 'bathroom' the council doesn't have to be any the wiser, if you catch my drift."

For a moment, Tex eyed his neighbor, his sense of injustice piqued to such an extent that he momentarily wondered if Alec would consider death by lawnmower an act of self-defense or not. But then wiser councils prevailed. He sighed and said, "Okay. A free pass for you and Marcie to use my new bathroom."

Ted pumped the air with his fist. "Yesss," he said, then added, "What about mine and Marcie's folks?"

"Don't push it, Ted."

Ted immediately relented. He must have seen the fire in Tex's eye. "No, of course. You're absolutely right. Gotta keep it exclusive. Neighbors only."

Tex watched Ted toddle off in the direction of the house and shook his head. So much for building a discreet bathroom and no one finding out about it. Soon the whole town would know, Ted being the inveterate blabbermouth that he was.

"Oh, darn," he said, his sense of excitement having taken a considerable hit.

CHAPTER 6

$\mathcal{V}$esta walked in through the sliding glass door and into her granddaughter's living room. Even though she enjoyed these conversations with her son-in-law, what she enjoyed even more was to spend time with the latest addition to the Poole family roster.

"And how is my sweetheart?" she said as she leaned over the crib and took a closer gander at baby Grace.

"Asleep," said Odelia curtly. "And I'd appreciate it if you didn't wake her up, Gran."

"Oh, I won't wake her up, I promise," said Vesta as she marveled at this clear evidence that God was still in his heaven and that all was well with the world. "Isn't she just gorgeous?" she whispered. "Isn't she the most gorgeous baby you've ever laid eyes on?"

"Yes, she is," said Odelia. "Now stop crowding her and sit down."

"I'm not crowding her," said Vesta. "I'm just admiring her." She took a load off her feet and dropped down on the couch next to her grandchild. "What, no cats?" she asked, glancing around. Usually Max and Dooley and the others couldn't stay away from Odelia.

"They've been awfully quiet," said Odelia. "Ever since Grace was born they've been walking on eggshells."

"Which is a good thing, no? Making sure they don't disturb the baby?"

"Yeah, but it's more than that. It's as if they still don't know how to deal with the fact that this little family of two is now suddenly a little family of three."

"And soon to be a little family of four?" Vesta cheekily inquired.

"Let's wait and see how it goes with Grace," said Odelia. "I'm not sure I'm dealing with this new situation all that well myself, to be perfectly honest."

"Oh, you're dealing with it just wonderfully. You're a born mother, honey." She patted her granddaughter's knee. "Have you heard the latest? Tex has hired me to manage his spa. Isn't that just great? And I have to say I'm bubbling with plans for the new addition."

Odelia frowned at her. "New spa? What are you talking about?"

"The new spa he's building in his backyard. Poole Spa & Pool. I coined the name, of course. Gotta have a catchy name." She sighed with relish. "It's going to be just great. First we'll open her up to the neighborhood, of course, but if things go well, I think we might be able to service the entire town. Which means money will be flowing into the family coffers and before you know it we'll all be rich!"

"How can Dad build a pool in his backyard? He doesn't have the space."

"Oh, he's going to take over some of the land behind us."

"He's buying the land from Blake Carrington? I didn't know he was selling."

"We're going to need plenty of parking space, of course, and dressing rooms, and a kiddie pool. Oh, this is exactly what this family needs right now: a project we can all tackle together. Marge will give up her job at the library, and Tex will drop his doctor's practice. And you're practically out of the *Gazette* anyway…" She gave Odelia a thoughtful look. "I was thinking about offering Chase the pool guard job, though maybe if we build a fitness club he could be our resident fitness instructor instead. Do you think he'd drop his career as a cop for that?"

Odelia had been staring at her with open-mouthed admiration and Vesta couldn't help but experience a sense of pride that she was putting her family on the map like this.

"It's all because of Grace, of course," she said, smoothing her tracksuit pants. "I was thinking we need to create a legacy, you know. And wellness is always going to be big business." She glanced over to the crib where Grace was still sleeping peacefully. "I can just see her now. Grace Kingsley: General Manager of Poole Spa & Pool. Though if her name had been Grace Poole it would have been even better, of course. Brand recognition is very important in this business." She frowned. "Do you think Chase would mind if Grace took the Poole name instead? Mh?"

"Gran! Are you nuts!"

"Shh," she said, placing a finger to her lips. "The baby."

"God," Odelia said, shaking her head for some reason.

Just then, the cats walked in through the pet flap, one after the other: Max, Dooley, Harriet and Brutus. Single file, like a procession of cats. They looked solemn, Vesta thought, as if they had something on their minds. She couldn't think what it could be but she had a feeling they would soon find out.

The cat procession halted in front of them and Max was the first to speak.

"Odelia," he said. "Gran. We have an important question for you."

"Shoot," said Vesta, hoping they wouldn't kick up a fuss about the pool. She knew that cats don't like water, and her cats were no exception. All they'd have to do was to steer clear of the pool area. Or better yet: maybe they could steer clear of the spa entirely. No customer visiting a spa likes to be confronted with a bunch of cats roaming around. It just gives a bad impression. Unprofessional.

"It's come to our attention," said Max, looking very serious as he spoke, "that you've stopped working as a police consultant. It's also come to our attention that you no longer work for the *Gazette*. Which means you no longer need us to do your legwork and act as your eyes and ears. In other words," the voluminous cat concluded, "Our job description seems to have gone through a fundamental change."

"Well put," said Vesta. But then Max always did have a way with words.

"But if we're not spies anymore," said Max, "then what are we?"

"What Max means to say," said Harriet, "is this: what do we do?"

"Excellent question," said Vesta. She turned to her grand-daughter, curious how she would respond. In fact all eyes now turned to Odelia: four pairs of cat eyes and Vesta's.

Odelia smiled. "Look, you guys. It's true that I'm not a police consultant right now, since I'm on leave, which means you can all take a well-deserved break."

Dooley's mouth opened and closed a few times, and it was clear that Odelia's response wasn't what the cats had expected.

"A break?" said Harriet finally.

"Yeah, a vacation," Odelia clarified.

"Like a holiday," Vesta further explained.

"A holiday," Max murmured, as if the concept was alien to him.

"Odelia is absolutely right," said Vesta. "This is a time to rejoice. With baby Grace having joined our family, and me becoming the new General Manager of the Poole Spa & Pool a new era has begun. And so you can all take a nice long vacation." She threw up her arms. "Let's have some fun, for crying out loud!"

A loud wail rose up from baby Grace's crib. Looked like she was all for fun!

CHAPTER 7

"Max?"

"Mh?"

"I'm bored."

"Me, too, Dooley," I said with a sigh.

"I'm also bored," said Brutus with an even deeper sigh.

"I don't get this," said Harriet. "It's just one little baby. And suddenly everything is completely different? How is that even possible?"

Just for a change of scenery, we'd all relocated to the front yard, where we now lay, doing some pet watching and generally having a lazy old time. But even though Gran had insisted we have some fun and enjoy an extended vacation, it wasn't long before all four of us were bored out of our tiny skulls.

"I read somewhere that having a baby changes people's perceptions," said Brutus, causing us all to look in his direction with wonder written all over our features.

"You *read* that?" I asked, much surprised that Brutus would out himself as a *reader,* of all things.

"Yeah, online," he said, ignoring our visible astonishment.

"When humans have a baby suddenly the way they look at the world and their own life goes through a fundamental change. Instead of everything revolving around them and their ambitions and likes and dislikes, the kid now comes first. And so it's not surprising that Odelia decides to chuck everything and put Grace's wellbeing in first place." He gave a weary shake of the head. "Which means we're all screwed, you guys. No more mysteries, no more exciting car chases, no more *danger*."

"To be fair, we were never in any car chases," I said. "Or in any real danger."

"Oh, there's been plenty of danger," said Harriet. "Remember that time we were locked inside the walls of that creepy old mansion? That was very dangerous. And I can't count on the digits of one paw the many times Odelia had to be saved from the clutches of some creepy killer."

Brutus glanced in my direction. "You saved her a couple of times, if memory serves."

"As a matter of fact, I did," I said, my claws tingling at the memory.

"That's all in the past from now on, you guys," said Dooley sadly.

"Yeah, no more brushes with death," I said wistfully.

"No more 'Elementary, my dear Dooley,'" said Dooley.

"Ah, well," I said. "Maybe it's all for the best."

"Yeah, we had a good run, didn't we?" said Brutus.

"We had an excellent run," Harriet chimed in. "And maybe now I'll finally be able to focus on my singing career. All this catching killers is all fine and dandy, but there's more to life than murder and mayhem." She gave her right paw a tentative lick, then brushed it across her noble visage. "There's music and lights and dancing and... show biz!"

"Lady Gaga made another movie," Brutus pointed out. "And if she can do it, so can you, sweetie pie."

"Of course I could," said Harriet, perking up. "First I'll build a phenomenal singing career, create a string of hits, get a Hollywood agent, and then it's movie stardom for me!"

Stranger things have happened, of course, and I just wanted to point out that Harriet's singing was still a darn sight better than ninety percent of the current crop of pop stars, when suddenly a cab drew up in front of the house and a fat man practically rolled out. He had a shaggy mop of blond hair that reminded me of a poodle and was dressed in a loud Hawaiian T-shirt and pink Bermudas. He also had a tiny sort of dog in his arms and glanced in our direction with a look of confusion. Behind him, a second person alighted. She was a female of indefinite age with a face like a horse and a lot of teeth. She, too, was clutching a smallish species of canine and looked up at the house with a puzzled expression.

"Are you sure this is the place?" she asked the cab driver, who was busy excavating a large number of suitcases from the back of his vehicle.

"Yup, this is where Odelia Poole lives," said the cab driver. "I personally know the Pooles and I can verify that this is the right place." He pointed to Marge and Tex's house. "Tex Poole is my doctor and he lives right there. Once, a couple of years ago, I was suffering from itchy feet and even though it was the middle of the night, Doc Poole greeted me with all the cordiality of an old friend." He smiled at the recollection. "I'll never forget what he told me when I pulled off my socks. 'Smells like a ripe French cheese, Norbert. The stinky kind.' Ah, those were the days." He slammed the trunk of the cab shut and stood in wait for his fee.

The fat man with the blond bob dutifully took out his wallet and did the honors, while the horsy lady stood gaping at the four of us with distinct dismay. "Cats," she said disapprovingly. "Tessa didn't say anything about cats."

"Well, looks like this is us," said the large man in a jolly voice. "Now let's hope this Odelia Poole person is home."

"Odelia Kingsley," I pointed out. "Odelia took Chase's name."

The tiniest of the two tiny dogs studied me closely, then said, "Are you the lord of the manor, cat?"

"The name is Max," I said. "And yes, this is my home."

"Our home," Harriet corrected me. "Who are you?"

The doggie licked its lips, then blinked and said, "Little John."

"So who is Big John?" asked Brutus.

The doggie gestured to the large man who was carrying his compatriot. "That guy over there."

"And my name is Little Janine," the other little doggie squeaked. "I was named after my human, whose name is Janine."

"I hate to be rude," I said, "but what exactly are you doing here?"

Both doggies smiled down at me from their respective perches in their humans' arms. "We're going to live here from now on!" Little John cried happily.

"We're all going to be brothers and sisters!" Little Janine added for good measure.

CHAPTER 8

⚜

$\mathcal{B}$ig John dutifully rang the front doorbell and we all waited with bated breath for what was to follow. Dooley and Harriet and Brutus and myself because the news that four would suddenly become six had struck us hard. It wasn't the first time that visitors had arrived unexpectedly in our midst and stuck around for a while, but if Little John and Little Janine were to be believed, they were here to stay!

"I don't understand, Max," said Dooley. "Who are these people?"

"I have absolutely no idea, Dooley," I said.

The door swung open and Odelia appeared. Her face was flushed and she had that excited look in her eyes she always gets when she's nervous. "Welcome, welcome!" she cried, a little too loud, I thought. "Welcome to my humble home!"

"Why, thank you," said Big John. "So we have arrived at the home of Odelia Poole then? You are, in fact, her? I mean to say, you are she? In other words, you are *the* Odelia Poole?"

"Yes, I'm the Odelia," said Odelia. "Though it's Odelia Kingsley now."

"Kingsley?" asked Big John. "Who's Kingsley?"

"My husband, Chase Kingsley."

"Oh, righto. Well, I'm John Boggles, and this is my wife Janine. Though you can call me Big John—everybody else does," he added magnanimously.

"Just call me Janine," said Janine, giving her husband the look of a much-put-upon wife. "Thanks for taking us in, Odelia. Tessa said you once saved her life, and since we felt we had nowhere else to go…"

"Oh, of course," said Odelia, darting a quick glance to the two dogs, then directing a look down to the four of us, who were still drinking in the scene with interest. She stepped back and Big John and his better half disappeared inside.

And since there was nothing to be gained by remaining on the sidelines, we followed suit. This was one conversation we did not want to miss.

"I have to admit Tessa took me somewhat by surprise," said Odelia. "And so as far as sleeping arrangements go, I haven't fully worked out the, um, the details."

"Just put us anywhere," said Big John. "We're not fussy, are we, sweetums?"

"As long as we have a bed to sleep in, we're perfectly happy," Janine confirmed.

"I guess you'd like to freshen up a little first?" Odelia suggested.

"Yes, that would be lovely," said Janine. "We flew here straight from the continent, where we were staying with some friends in Bucharest, but unfortunately the tabloids managed to track us down and decided to organize a vigil in front of my friend's house, so we couldn't possibly stay."

Odelia swallowed uneasily. "You don't think… they will follow you here?"

Big John shrugged his big shoulders. "In life nothing is certain, Miss Poole."

"Mrs. Kingsley," Janine corrected her helpmeet.

"But we will muddle through, I can assure you."

"I don't think we were followed," said Janine. "And Tessa is the only one who knows where we are right now. Even our families have no idea we flew to the States."

"It's a sad state of affairs when the head of a nation has to go into hiding," said Big John with a sigh as he took in his surroundings. He homed in on the sliding glass door, through which the backyard was visible. "Oh, this is nice," he said. "Very homey, I must say."

Just then, Grace decided that the conversation could use the benefit of her personal contribution, and she opened her throat to loudly intervene.

"Oh, will you look at this cutie-pie!" said Janine, and for the next ten minutes or so, Grace was the center of attention, as had in fact been the case ever since she'd joined our ranks.

In order to fully benefit from the Grace Experience, Big John and his wife had put down their pets, and Little John and Little Janine now tripped up to us. After engaging in some sniffing action—why dogs enjoy sniffing butts so much will always be a mystery to me—they settled down, tails wagging and tongues lolling.

"So what do you guys do around here for fun?" asked Little John.

"We loiter," said Brutus dryly.

"No, we don't, smoochie poo," said Harriet. "We sing, we dance, we live!"

"We eat, we drink, we poo, we pee," said Dooley.

"And then we do it all over again," I added.

"In other words, pretty much what we do," said Little John.

"At least when we're not hobnobbing with world leaders," Little Janine supplied.

"You hobnob with world leaders?" asked Harriet, much impressed.

"Of course. Big John is Prime Minister of England. He runs an entire country. So it's only natural that he would frequently meet other prime ministers, and presidents, and even kings and queens. All in a day's work for him—and us."

"How is he going to run his country when he's staying with us?" I asked.

"Well…" Little Janine directed a hesitant look at Little John. "Let's just say Big John is temporarily indisposed because of circumstances beyond his control."

"Things have gotten a little heated on the home front," said Little John. "So Big John and Janine felt it wise to lay low for a while. Let things cool off, you see."

Frankly I didn't see, but since these two were now guests in our home, I felt it was probably rude to pry. So instead I decided to give them the grand tour… which took us about five seconds, since our home is admittedly a tiny one.

"Lovely," Little Janine finally murmured politely. "Absolutely lovely."

"It isn't much," I said. "But it's home."

"And we love it," said Harriet.

"Though we love our own home even more, don't we, sunshine?" said Brutus.

"Your own home?" asked Little Janine. "Do you mean to say you don't actually live here?"

"No, me and Harriet live next door," said Brutus. "And so does Dooley. Only Max lives here—officially, at least."

And since both dogs stared at me in wonder, I decided to give them the lowdown on the Poole family setup. "Odelia is my human, so I live with her. Dooley's human is Odelia's grandmother, who lives with Tex and Marge next door.

Harriet belongs to Marge, and Brutus…" I frowned. "Who do you belong to again, Brutus?"

"Officially I belong to Chase," said Brutus, "after Chase's mom gave me to him for safekeeping. But since Harriet and I are an item, I actually live next door."

"And since Max and I are besties," Dooley said, "I usually hang out here."

Little John blinked. "Hard to keep track."

"Oh, it's not all that complicated," I said. "We actually consider both homes as one home, and come and go as we please. It's all very mellow and friendly. The Poole way, you know."

"I like it," said Little Janine, perking up a little. "I think we're going to feel right at home… in your homes."

"My case is your case," said Dooley.

"What Dooley means to say," I said, "is that *mi casa es su casa*."

"That's what I said!"

CHAPTER 9

I honestly felt as if my 'little home' was getting a little too crowded for comfort, and so I decided to do the only thing that seemed sensible: flee!

And since my friends all felt the same way, we quickly made ourselves scarce by means of that wonderful invention: the pet flap.

"Phew," said Harriet once we were outside again. "That was a close call."

"A close call?" said Dooley with a touch of concern. "What do you mean?"

"Isn't it obvious?" asked Brutus. "Odelia's house has just been taken over by the enemy, Dooley. From now on Little John and Little Janine are in charge. So if I were you, I'd find myself a new place to call home."

"Would you call dogs the enemy?" I asked.

"Of course! Dogs are our mortal enemy. Every cat knows this."

"But what about Fifi?" I asked. "She's not the enemy."

"Obviously Fifi is the exception that proves the rule."

"I don't actually consider Fifi a dog," said Harriet.

"Me, neither," said Brutus. "To me Fifi is an honorary cat."

"Exactly! And so is Rufus. They were probably both cats in a previous life."

And these deep thoughts dispensed with, Harriet and Brutus skedaddled.

"I'm scared, Max," Dooley confessed, and he actually looked scared.

"No need to be scared, Dooley," I said. Then: "What are you scared about?"

"Our home isn't our home anymore! It's now in the hands of the enemy!"

"I'm sure Little John and Little Janine aren't actually the enemy," I said soothingly. "In fact they struck me as a very polite and friendly pair of dogs."

"But they're dogs, Max. Dogs! Taking over our home!"

"They're not actually taking over our home as much as visiting it." Though to be honest I had no idea whether this was actually true or not. After all, no mention had been made of an expiration date to this surprise visit. As far as I knew, Big John and his entourage might settle down in Hampton Cove indefinitely.

But instead I said, "I'm sure they won't stick around for very long. After all, Big John is the Prime Minister of England, Dooley. And how long can a Prime Minister run his country through Zoom calls? At some point he has to go back. Right?"

But Dooley's look of distinct concern told me he was the wrong cat to ask.

"I think they're here to stay, Max," my friend said. "Forever and ever and ever."

And as Dooley and I were discussing the uncertain future we were facing, suddenly I had the feeling we were being observed. But when I looked around, I couldn't see anyone or anything that could be the cause of this sensation. Still, my

41

skin was crawling, which happens every time I'm under close scrutiny.

"What's wrong, Max?" Dooley immediately asked.

"Nothing," I said, not wanting to alarm my friend any further. "Nothing at all."

And that's when it happened. A loud scream rent the air. It was Harriet!

"You creep!" her voice cried out. "You horrible, horrible creep!"

Immediately Dooley and I hurried in the direction of the rose bushes, Harriet and Brutus's favorite spot in Odelia's backyard. It's nice and shady there—and very discreet, if you know what I mean.

And as we approached, suddenly a man came hurrying out of those same bushes. He was big and hulking and was dressed in a long dark coat. He was also wearing sunglasses, which struck me as ominous, since those rose bushes are impenetrable to the sun's rays, no matter how hard she tries. Those same sunglasses stood at an angle on his nose, as if they'd taken a hit, and I could count at least three long scratches across his nose, which was red and bleeding.

"And next time you assault a lady, I hope you'll think again!" Harriet said as a verbal parting gift to the strange and dangerous-looking individual.

"What happened?" I asked the moment we joined our friends.

"That man," said Harriet, her paw to her chest, "stepped on my tail!"

"No, he didn't," said Dooley, visibly shocked to the core.

"Willfully!" Harriet cried as she raised her paw and placed it across her brow. She'd closed her eyes and was acting the part of the dainty diva to perfection.

"So I scratched him," said Brutus.

"Oh, my brave hero," said Harriet.

"And then I scratched him again."

"My knight in shining armor!"

"No one," said Brutus, a tremor in his voice, "touches my lady in anger!"

"My noble Lancelot!" Harriet trilled, and held out her paw.

"There, there," said Brutus, taking the fin and patting it fervently.

And while Harriet recovered from her terrible ordeal, I glanced in every direction, but try as I might, I couldn't detect a single trace of the intruder.

"I wonder what he was doing here," I murmured as I studied the spot where the man had stood. Mother nature, when creating the man, certainly hadn't stinted on shoe size, that was obvious from the indentations in the topsoil.

"I'll bet he's Papa Razzi," said Dooley.

"You mean a paparazzo," I said.

"Him, too," said Dooley with a shiver.

"It's possible," I admitted. Perhaps the same tabloid reporters who had been hounding Big John before had managed to track him down and were ready to do what they did best: catch him in unflattering outfits and turn him into a national laughingstock. It was, apparently, why he had selected our home as his hideaway.

"This is all very worrying, Max," said Dooley. "I'm very worried."

"Yeah, it's not conducive to a peaceful atmosphere," I said.

"It could be a kidnapper," Brutus suggested, now that Harriet had been sufficiently consoled. "Out to nab baby Grace. There are gangs that steal babies on commission. Or they could be wanting to kidnap her and hold her for ransom."

"Oh, no!" said Harriet. "Not baby Grace! Max, you have to do something!"

Brutus looked a little perturbed at the mention of my name. "Or I could do something," he pointed out.

"Of course, twinkle toes," said Harriet sweetly. "But since Odelia is Max's human, and Grace is Odelia's baby, Max is probably best placed to save her."

"Mh," said Brutus, clearly not in full agreement with this specious reasoning.

"We better see if Grace is still there," I said, and moved off in the direction of the house. My friends all followed me, and moments later we were passing through the pet flap and into the house proper, making a beeline for Grace's crib. And as we hopped up onto the table to take a closer look, much to our satisfaction she was still happily gurgling away, looking as pink and cherubic as usual.

"Phew," I said, and probably spoke for all of us.

Odelia, who'd just returned from upstairs, where she'd been overseeing sleeping arrangements for the Boggles, started a little when she saw us all hovering over the crib. "What's wrong?" she immediately asked as she joined us.

"We saw a man in the bushes," said Dooley. "And he attacked Harriet. We think he might be a kidnapper. And so we wanted to see if he kidnapped Grace or not."

"Oh, dear," said Odelia, bringing a distraught hand to her face. "Are you all right, Harriet?"

"My tail still hurts," said Harriet. "And if Brutus hadn't fought him off, things could have turned really nasty. I could see it in his eyes. Evil, Odelia. Pure evil!"

"He could be part of a gang of baby snatchers," said Brutus. "I heard there's one active in the neighborhood. Snatching babies and selling them for parts."

"People don't sell babies for parts, Brutus," said Odelia.

"Yeah, you're thinking of cars," I said.

"Maybe they want to eat them?" Harriet suggested. "I read

on Facebook that there are people out there that like to eat babies. Like a Snickers bar, you know."

"Don't believe everything you read on Facebook, Harriet," said Odelia. But I could tell that the story of this tall, dark stranger in the bushes had rattled her.

"I just wish I'd knocked him out when I had the chance," said Brutus grimly.

"You're much too nice, wuggle bear," said Harriet. "That's your problem."

"I know, I know. I had him in my paws but I let him go. Darn it!"

"Can you give me a description?" asked Odelia.

"I can do you one better," said Brutus, expanding his chest. He held out his paw. "You can scrape some of his DNA from my claws and have Chase run it through the database."

"Oh, love muffin!" Harriet cried. "You're so clever!"

"One does one's best," said Brutus modestly.

"I'll carefully scrape off some of that DNA from your claws, Brutus," said Odelia, "so Chase has something to work with." And she proceeded in the direction of the staircase to retrieve what is commonly termed a cotton swab. Humans use it to poke around in their ears—the reason is entirely unclear to me, but then we all know humans are a very strange species. If someone tried to poke me in the ear with a cotton swab they'd get quite an earful, I can promise you.

But before Odelia could equip herself with the necessary DNA-retrieval tools, suddenly John Boggles appeared in the stairwell, almost bumping into our human. "Oh," said Odelia, a little startled. "I was just going to—"

And she probably would have said more, but just at that moment Harriet started screaming at the top of her voice— quite the performance, I must say.

"It's the man!" she shrieked. "Brutus—get him!"

And true enough: the mystery man who had appeared,

then disappeared from the bushes, was staring at us through the sliding glass door!

"It's the kidnapper!" Odelia cried, and grabbed for the first available weapon that she found, in this case a smallish statuette of Minnie Mouse Gran had once gifted her.

"What's going on?" asked Big John, much perturbed.

"This man is here to kidnap my daughter!" Odelia said as she took a firmer grip on the makeshift weapon. The wannabe kidnapper had now placed both hands next to his face, and his face flat against the window, his damaged schnozz greasing up the glass, in an obvious attempt to look inside.

"The nerve of the guy!" said Brutus. "He's simply blatant!"

And then the most astonishing thing happened: like a man possessed with nerves of steel, John Boggles stepped to the fore, like the fearless leader that he was, yanked open the door and... clapped Harriet's attacker on the back!

"Anything to report, Wilkins?" he asked.

"No, sir. Looks like the coast is clear."

"Good man," said Big John, and Wilkins tipped an imaginary cap, then removed himself from the scene, presumably to invade some other home!

"What just happened?" asked Harriet.

"Do you know that man?" asked Odelia.

"Mh?" said Big John absentmindedly. "Oh, you mean Wilkins? Yes, of course. He's my PPO. Goes with me wherever I go. Makes sure nobody blows me up or shoots me or some such tomfoolery."

"PPO?"

"Personal protection officer. Works for the Metropolitan Police."

"Is that like that golden robot from Star Wars, Max?" asked Dooley.

"I think he's called C-3PO, Dooley," I said.

"But, but, but..." Odelia stuttered.

"I know, I know," said Big John. "I didn't like it myself at first. Took me a while to get used to. But now I find it has a sort of soothing effect, don't you know. A kind of reassurance that the world is a safe place as long as Wilkins is around."

"I thought he was here to kidnap my daughter," said Odelia, still much shaken.

"Wilkins? Oh, no," said Big John with a light chuckle. "I can assure you kidnapping babies is the last thing on his mind. He's a perfectly honorable chappie. Heart of gold and all that. Won plenty of medals, don't you know." He glanced around until his eye settled on the couch. "Would you perhaps be so kind to provide Wilkins with a pillow and some sheets? I'm sure he'd love nothing better than to sleep on the cold, hard floor, but I believe in treating my staff well."

"Of course," said Odelia, looking a little sandbagged as she replaced the statuette on the kitchen counter, then mounted the stairs to fetch some bedding for Wilkins.

Brutus, who was still holding up his paw, asked, "So what about the DNA?"

"I think you can put your paw down now, Brutus," I said. "The value of that particular DNA has just taken a big hit and is now trading at cents on the dollar."

CHAPTER 10

*J*ust move in with us—just do it," Brutus
suggested.

"I don't know, Brutus," I said.

"Look, it's obvious that Odelia has other things on her mind right now: the baby, and now these friends of hers with their dogs and their... stuff. Time for you and Dooley to move out and move in with us. Plenty of space for the four of us!"

It was a tempting offer, of course, and Brutus had a point. Odelia did have a lot of things on her mind, and she certainly didn't have time to deal with Dooley and me. Case in point: she'd forgotten to fill up our bowls, which was a first, and to clean out our litter boxes, which was an unpleasant surprise. Also, Little John and Little Janine had confiscated my favorite blanket. All in all, a sad state of affairs!

"But where will we sleep?" asked Dooley.

"That's the easy part: you and Max will sleep on Gran's bed and Harriet and me will sleep where we sleep now: on Marge and Tex's bed. Easy peasy!"

Tempting, very tempting indeed.

We had escaped from the house, which was far too busy and noisy to our liking, and had decided to avoid the backyard, just in case more men in black jumped out at us and tried to kidnap us—or, as the case may be, stepped on our tails—and were now enjoying the peace and quiet of Marge and Tex's backyard.

"I think it's the perfect solution," said Brutus, reiterating his point. "After all, cats are survivors. When things become too hectic or too uncomfortable for our taste, we simply move on. In that sense we show our superiority to the canine species, who stick to their humans like glue, come rain or shine."

"Cats don't stick to their humans like glue?" asked Dooley.

"No, of course not, silly. We go where life takes us. Free spirits to the core." He looked up when Harriet came walking out through the pet flap. "And?" he said hopefully.

"Beef," said Harriet sadly.

"What, again? We had beef yesterday, and the day before."

"I know. I told Marge and she's going shopping tomorrow."

"Tomorrow!" He sagged a little. "Oh, well. I guess these little setbacks are life's way of making us more spiritual." He returned his attention to us. "Now where was I? Oh, that's right. I was explaining the essential sense of adventure and independence of the feline species. We don't need anyone or anything."

"Are you moving in with us?" asked Harriet.

"We're thinking about it," I said.

"Just do it," was her advice. "It's not your fault that Odelia decided to replace you with a baby, and then started filling the house with her dubious friends. So it's not a lot of fun. I say deal with it. If life deals you lemons, make lemonade."

"I don't like lemonade," Dooley murmured sadly.

"Odelia didn't exactly replace us with a baby," I said.

"No, she said she would always have a place for us in her home," said Dooley, on whom this conversation was having a slightly disconcerting effect, judging from the way he was darting anxious glances to me from time to time.

"You have to understand humans speak with forked tongues," said Brutus.

"Odelia's tongue is forked?!" Dooley asked, thoroughly shocked.

"Not literally, of course," said Brutus curtly. "I was just trying to make a point. Humans often say one thing and do the opposite. They're afraid that if they tell you the truth you'll kick up a fuss. So instead they feed you some convenient lie, and then do whatever they intended to do anyway, hoping you won't notice."

I frowned at our butch black friend. "So you're saying... What are you saying, exactly?"

"He's saying that Odelia is sick and tired of having a pair of cats infest her home," said Harriet. "Especially with Grace to take care of. So she invited these Boggles and their canine appendages to drive you both out of the house."

"Oh, dear," I said. It was true that our home wasn't our home anymore. Not with two human Boggles and two canine Boggles having taken over. And then of course there was Grace, who seemed to find a perverse pleasure in interrupting our precious and sacred nap time by imitating a fire engine at regular intervals.

"So you're saying this was a deliberate strategy by Odelia to get rid of us?"

"Of course!" said Brutus. "And a very clever one, too. Now she can blame everything on the Boggles, and you have no other recourse but to move out."

"My theory," said Harriet, lowering her voice to a

conspiratorial whisper, "is that Odelia turned her home into an Airbnb and the Boggles are her first guests."

"What's an Airbnb?" asked Dooley.

"It's like a bed and breakfast in a private home," I said. "To be booked online."

"At least over here things are still the way they've always been," said Harriet as she smoothed her whiskers. "And since Marge is too old to have babies, and so is Gran, I think it's safe to say that this haven of peace and hospitality is a given."

Just then, Tex came walking out of the house. For some reason he was wearing a yellow hard hat on top of his head, and was dressed in a high-vis vest over blue coveralls. He was also carrying what looked like a sledgehammer and had a look of determination in his eyes. And as he approached the garden house, we all followed his progress with marked interest.

"What's up with Tex?" I asked.

"I have absolutely no idea," said Brutus. "He did mention something about a second bathroom this morning, though I told him he could always use my litter box. As usual, he ignored me, of course."

"He ignores you because he doesn't understand you, angel," said Harriet.

"And I think he can understand us perfectly," said Brutus. "He's been married to Marge for twenty-five years—plenty of time to pick up our language. No, he's simply pretending not to understand us because it's more convenient to him."

"How do you figure that?" I asked.

"If he doesn't understand us, he can ignore us," Brutus explained. "And if he ignores us, he doesn't have to clean out our litter box, fill up our bowls, or take us to the vet when we're dealing with some medical emergency. It's laziness, pure and simple."

"I don't know if…" I began to say, but Brutus held up his paw.

"You don't have to teach me humans, Max. They're a duplicitous species. Just look at Odelia. Promising to take care of you forever, and the moment a couple of Boggles arrive she's suddenly forgotten you even exist."

"All she did was forget to fill our bowls," I said.

"And forget to clean out our litter boxes. And don't forget she gave your favorite blanket to the Boggles," said Dooley.

"She didn't actually give my blanket to the Boggles, Dooley," I said. "They simply took it."

"Because Odelia took her eye off the ball," Brutus said.

"What ball?" asked Dooley. "I thought we were talking about a blanket."

"What *is* that man up to?" said Harriet now.

We all returned our attention to Tex, and suddenly, and much to our shock and horror, he heaved that sledgehammer high over his head… and smashed the door of his own garden house!

"He's gone crazy!" Brutus cried. "The man has gone cuckoo!"

"It's true," said Harriet in hushed tones. "Tex has gone bananas."

And they were absolutely right: the good doctor was smashing in that garden house as if it had personally insulted him. The wood splintered, the windows cracked, and soon an entire wall of the structure collapsed under the onslaught!

"This is gratuitous violence on an alarming scale," said Harriet, shaking her head.

"But why!" Dooley cried. "Why is he doing this!"

"I've read about this," said Brutus. "Human men of a certain age sometimes go through something called a midlife crisis. It makes them go all weird."

"I thought men suffering from a midlife crisis started wearing a leather jacket and bought themselves a Harley-Davidson," I said.

"Or started dating a woman young enough to be their daughter," Harriet said.

"A midlife crisis manifests itself in different ways in different people," said Brutus, our resident Sigmund Freud. "And in Tex it apparently manifests as a desire to destroy innocent garden houses that have never done anything wrong."

We watched on as a second wall of the garden house now collapsed, and Tex started in on wall number three. The roof was already dangling at a crooked angle, and if this kept up, soon there would be no more garden house left!

"I don't feel safe, Max," Dooley intimated in a soft tone. "What if he starts destroying the house? And then Odelia's house? We won't have a home anymore!"

"Dooley is right," said Harriet. "We have to stop him before he destroys the house!"

"Oh, God," said Brutus. "This is just an appetizer for Tex, isn't it? A dress rehearsal. The moment that garden house is gone he'll come for our home!"

"We better tell Marge," said Harriet. "She's the only one who can stop this *madness*!"

And so we all ran into the house, popping through that pet flap one after the other, then spread out to look for the lady of the manor. If anyone could stop Terminator Tex, it was Marge!

"Marge!" I called out as I skipped into the living room.

"Marge!" I could hear Dooley yelling as he checked the upstairs bedroom.

"Marge, where are you!" Brutus called down into the basement.

"Marge, your husband has gone completely stark raving mad!" Harriet yelled.

But unfortunately of Marge there was no trace.

We gathered in the kitchen. "Maybe she's gone into hiding," Harriet suggested.

"Maybe Tex locked her up in the attic," was Brutus's opinion.

"Maybe Tex chopped her up into little pieces and stuffed her into the freezer!" Dooley cried.

But just then, and much to our elation, Gran walked into the kitchen and went straight to the fridge.

"Gran!" Dooley practically screamed, causing the old lady to jump.

"Dooley, you startled me!" she said, clutching a hand to her chest.

"It's Tex," said Harriet. "He's lost his mind."

"Tell me something I don't know," said Gran as she stuck her head in the fridge and started rummaging around for something to eat.

"No, but he's really lost his mind," I said. "He's taking a sledgehammer to the garden house and completely demolishing it!"

"Of course he is," said Gran with infuriating equanimity. "How else is he going to build our new spa?" She retracted her head and fixed us with a kindly look. "When you want to make an omelet, you have to break some eggs. Hasn't anyone ever told you that?"

"Is Tex making an omelet?" asked Dooley with a puzzled frown.

"No, but he's creating our family's newest venture: the Poole Spa & Pool, of which I'm the proud General Manager. So rejoice, ladies and gentlemen, for a new era of wealth and prosperity is about to commence. Within a few short months we'll all be rich!"

And with these surprising words, she stuck a piece of cold chicken between her dentures and walked out, leaving four cats in the throes of a very powerful emotion. An emotion that can only be described as utter and complete stupefaction.

CHAPTER 11

"The Poole Spa & Pool," said Brutus with a touch of reverence. "It does have a nice ring to it, doesn't it?"

"No, it does not," Harriet snapped. "It means they're going to turn our lovely little home into some kind of glitzy resort, Brutus! Like the Ritz or the Carlton!"

"I think it's actually the Ritz-Carlton," I said, but she ignored me.

"Odd," said Brutus. "I thought there were laws against constructing a resort in the middle of a residential area."

"Laws are there to be broken, sugar plum," said Harriet. "And remember who Tex's sister-in-law is."

She was right, of course. Marge's brother's girlfriend is town mayor, and probably wouldn't mind bending a few rules and issuing a building permit were a building permit wasn't strictly allowed. In that sense, Tex was on velvet. He could build his big spa resort and the town council wouldn't utter a word in protest.

Who was uttering a word in protest was Dooley. "So Tex and Marge are starting a giant resort," he said, "and Odelia is starting a bed and breakfast in the air, and, and… where does that leave us, you guys!"

It was a question that gave us all pause. I don't know if you know, but cats enjoy a sedentary life—a life of peace and quiet and fixed habits. In that sense you might even call us autistic. And as far as I know life in a spa is never very peaceful or very quiet or staid. Guests come and go all the time, and usually these places come equipped with a fitness club and a nail salon and sometimes even with a hotel so guests who come from farther afield can still enjoy the spa experience.

And so as we slunk out of the house once more, and found ourselves confronted with a sweaty Tex who stood leaning on his sledgehammer and eyeing his work of destruction with satisfaction, I have to say a sense of gloom wrapped itself around us like a wet blanket.

"It's the end of an era, my friends," Brutus spoke softly. "Our home is no longer our home."

"Yeah, it's official," Harriet chimed in. "The Pooles have finally gone nuts."

"Or they've become very smart," I said. "There's probably a lot of money to be made in the wellness industry, and maybe they're right to grab a piece of it."

"At the very least they could have told us what they were up to," said Harriet.

Brutus turned to his lady love. "Which proves my point exactly, sweetums. Humans are duplicitous. That's just the way they are. They simply can't help it."

"I think I'm going to be sick," said Dooley.

We plunked ourselves down on our haunches. "So now what?" asked Harriet. "What are we going to do?"

"We could wait and see how things pan out," I suggested. "It might take months to build this hotel and spa, and maybe it won't even be a great success."

"I don't know about you," said Brutus, "but I don't think I'd enjoy living on a building site. People messing about, digging holes and trampling us underfoot."

"Cats are very small," Dooley agreed. "We can easily be trampled underfoot."

"Do you think they'll tear down the house?" asked Harriet, glancing up at our lovely home. "They just built it and already they're going to demolish it again?"

"It's the way of the future, sweet pea," said Brutus sadly. "Progress has its price."

Just then, Marge came charging out of the house. She must have just arrived home and seen the work her husband had wrought. "Tex Poole!" she cried. "What do you think you're doing!"

"I'm tearing down the garden house?" he said hesitantly.

"But why! I thought we were going to turn it into a bathroom?"

"You can't install a bathroom in an old wooden shack like this, honey. Better to build the thing from scratch and make it nice and sturdy. Build it in brick."

"Oh," she said, taking his point of view on board and taking it for a spin. "Did you at least remove all of your tools and Ma's gardening equipment?"

The sheepish look on Tex's face told us everything we needed to know.

"Oh, Tex," Marge sighed, as she dug through the wreckage and liberated the lawnmower. It had taken a dent but still looked fairly functional. Clearly it was made of sterner stuff than the garden house itself.

And since Marge and Tex seemed to have some personal issues to work out, we decided to give them some space and take a look across the hedge. Cats are optimists, you see, and always hope for the best. Perhaps in our absence Odelia had seen the error of her ways and had uninvited the Boggles and sent them on their way?

But we'd only taken one step through the opening in the hedge that divides both backyards to find our hopes crushed: John Boggle was lying stretched out on Chase's favorite lounge chair, busily tapping a message on his phone, while his dog Little John was lying right next to him, looking very important.

"Oh, hey, cats," said Little John. "Just the guys I wanted to see. Tell me, who do I talk to around here to take me for my walk? At home it's usually some junior member of John's staff who handles that kind of thing. In the meantime I've taken the liberty of relieving myself in those bushes over there."

I heard a sharp intake of breath behind me, and knew that Harriet had added two and two together and had come to the conclusion that Little John had relieved himself in her precious rose bushes—her and Brutus's makeout spot!

"Oh, and since you're here, can you talk to management—whoever they are—and tell them to change the food in our bowls? I tried some of the stuff they have on offer and I have to say it's subpar to say the least. Absolutely subpar." He closed his eyes again and waved an airy paw. "That's all for now. Dismissed."

I could sense that Harriet was about to explode, and so decided to lead her away. After all, it wouldn't do to commit dogicide and have Big John leave a negative review in the process. Everyone knows that reviews are a big driver of sales, especially for a new startup like Odelia's Airbnb endeavor.

"Let's go," I said, and gently took Harriet by the paw and led her into the house.

"He… he peed in our rose bushes, smoochie poo," she told

Brutus as she staggered along, looking quite stricken. "Our happy place!"

"I know, snuggle bunny," said Brutus, looking equally affected. "I know."

"And I'll bet he pooped, too," said Dooley, adding his two cents.

CHAPTER 12

❧

Inside the house, we found Odelia sitting next to Grace's cradle, appearing moderately frazzled. Then again, I guess starting a new business venture from scratch takes a lot out of a person, especially when she's just had a baby, which, to all intents and purposes, must be a tough proposition for any human.

Grace, meanwhile, was expressing her opinion on the matter at hand—whatever it was—with customary gusto: she'd opened her lungs and once again was doing a great imitation of a fire engine—or a jumbo jet, as Fifi's human would have described it. She certainly had a great set of pipes. If I wasn't mistaken one day she'd give Céline, Mariah, Barbra and Adele a run for their money.

"Do you think Little John pooped in her crib?" said Dooley as we glanced up at our human, who also looked a little pooped.

"Oh, you guys?" said Little Janine, walking up to us from the kitchen. Her jaws were still moving, and I could see crumbs of what looked like the remnants of a gourmet meal on her chin. "I hope you don't mind, but I used the funny-looking latrine in the kitchen to do my business. I know Little John said to do it in the bushes but I told him I'm a lady, and ladies never do their business in the bushes."

"Did you… use my litter box?" I asked, suddenly feeling a little sick.

"I don't know what you call it," said Little Janine. "It's big and made of plastic and there's some kind of funny-smelling sand inside. Very nice. Oh, and if you don't mind, can you tell Odelia to get me a dog bed? We had to leave England in such a rush Janine forgot to bring mine. Mind you, I only sleep on a Queen Bee dog bed, the one with the genuine sheep wool. I have sensitive skin so I can't sleep on anything else I'm afraid." She gave a sort of wave in our direction. "That'll be all."

"What was that all about?" asked Odelia, who'd taken Grace from her crib and was gently rocking her in her arms.

"Little Janine wants you to buy her a Queen B dog bed made of real sheep wool," I said.

"And Little John said to tell you the food is super," said Dooley.

"Subpar, Dooley, not super," I corrected my friend.

"And also, Little John pooped in our rose bushes," said Harriet sadly.

"And Little Janine pooped in Max's litter box," Brutus supplied with a grin.

"Uh-huh?" said Odelia. "Is that a fact?"

I had the impression she hadn't really paid a lot of attention to what we said, and I now saw she had dark rings under her eyes, presumably from a lack of sleep. Cats sleep all the time, you see, in the sense that we take what we can get as far as sleep is concerned. Humans, on the other hand, have this fixed idea that they can only sleep at night, and when they don't, they simply go through their day like a somnambulist —or the walking dead, whatever the case may be.

"She looks tired, Max," said Dooley, who had noticed the same phenomenon.

"She looks exhausted," said Harriet.

"She looks dead on her feet," said Brutus.

"It's the Airbnb," I said. "It must be tough having to deal with these guests."

I know it was certainly tough on us. Harriet and Brutus's favorite spot would never be the same again—dog excrement leaves a particularly nasty smell that is very hard to get rid of. And also, it's hard to get in the mood for sweet luvin' when everything around you smells like dog poo. My litter box was most definitely ruined now and I probably would never be able to go again—what cat likes to go where a dog has gone before? Certainly not me! And if I wasn't mistaken Little Janine and her little brother Little John had eaten all of our food.

Proof of this was when Dooley returned from the kitchen moments later, having ventured there for a quick session of stress-eating, and cried, "They've eaten all of our food!"

"Of course they have," Brutus grunted.

"I thought they said they didn't like it!" said Dooley.

"Even people who are used to five-star restaurants like to go to McDonald's from time to time, Dooley," I said. When he simply stared at me, not comprehending, I explained, "If what Little John and Little Janine are used to can be described as five-star meals then the food we get is more akin to a McDonald's Happy Meal." When he still stared at me, puzzled, I explained even further, "We eat what your average gourmet would call comfort food, and even though comfort food isn't what a foodie would recommend, they still enjoy it when they can."

Dooley blinked, then reiterated, "but they ate all of our food, Max!"

I sighed. "Yes, Dooley. And I'm sure Odelia has plenty more in store."

We glanced up at Odelia in hopeful anticipation, but when she simply stared back at us with unseeing eyes, it was obvious that our food situation was dire.

Stomping feet on the stairwell told us that we were no longer alone—then again, when you're living in an Airbnb, are you ever truly alone?

Janine Boggle appeared, waving what looked like a pillowcase. "What kind of laundry detergent did you use to wash these, Odelia? They smell awful."

"Tide pods," said Odelia in a toneless voice.

"Well, I can tell you right now that John won't get a wink of sleep on these. He's allergic to all synthetic fragrances. You'll simply have to give them another wash. And the sheets, too, of course, and the mattress cover, while we're at it."

Odelia nodded, and Janine frowned. "Oh, and can you ask your daughter to keep her voice down. John is on a Zoom call, and all this screaming is making it hard for him to focus. Thanks!" she ended on a chipper tone, and was off again.

"Tough business, the Airbnb business," said Harriet, putting into words what we were all thinking.

The sliding glass door slid open and Marge walked in. Her face was flushed, presumably in the aftermath of her discussion with her builder husband. "I'm here," she announced, quite unnecessarily, I thought, for we could see she was there. "How is it going?"

"I'm so glad you came," said Odelia, getting up with some effort. "I don't know where my head's at."

"Your head is on your shoulders, silly," Dooley laughed, but Odelia hadn't heard, for Grace had once again decided to loudly voice her discontent. "Can you look after her for a while? John is on a Zoom call and he can't focus. Oh, and I have some beddings to wash." She frowned. "Do you have fragrance-free detergent?"

Marge gave her daughter an odd look. "Who are these people again?"

"Friends of Tessa Torrance and Prince Dante. John is Prime Minister of England and Janine is his wife."

"But… what are they doing here is what I'd like to know."

Odelia shrugged. "To be absolutely honest it's a mystery to me, too."

"Honey, are you sure you're up to this? I thought you were going to take it easy for a while? Enjoy those first weeks of blessed motherhood?"

"I thought so, too, but Tessa insisted ours was the best place for John and Janine right now, so…" She blew a strand of hair from her eyes.

"What does Chase say?"

"He doesn't know yet."

"Oh, dear."

"He's been so busy with this new case. I hadn't the heart to tell him. You know how he is. He'd drop his case and come running and that's the last thing I want."

"But—"

"I'll tell him when he gets here."

"All right," said Marge as she took Grace from Odelia's arms. "I guess you know best." Immediately the baby stopped wailing and was soon glancing around with distinct interest.

"Hey, baby," I said, waving at the newborn. "My name is Max and these are my friends: Dooley, Harriet and Brutus."

"Hi, tiny human," Brutus growled.

"She does have a name, you know," said Harriet, and smiled up at the baby. "Hey, Grace. Can you understand what we're saying? You are a Poole, aren't you?"

But baby Grace didn't speak. Instead, she drooled, which I guess is also a form of communication.

"Babies don't immediately start speaking," said Dooley knowingly. "I saw that on the Discovery Channel. It takes a couple of years."

"Years!" Harriet cried. "But why!"

"Because humans are slow," Brutus grunted. "Everybody knows that."

"Yeah, it takes them years to start talking, and years to start walking," said Dooley, "and years to start riding a bike, and years to start driving a car. It's a very, very, *very* slow process. Like watching paint dry."

"Give me kittens any day," Harriet murmured. "Much quicker on the uptake."

"And a lot cuter, too," Brutus grumbled.

"Would you call kittens cuter?" I said. I thought Grace looked pretty cute. All pink and round and shiny with health and vigor.

"Definitely," said Brutus. "Nothing beats kittens when it comes to the cuteness factor."

"I'm so tired," said Odelia, rubbing her face. "But if I lie down I know I'll fall asleep and wake up twelve hours from now."

"Give me those beddings," said Marge. "I have a load to wash anyway."

"No synthetic fragrances, though," said Odelia. "Or fabric softeners."

Marge rolled her eyes. "Between Tex demolishing our garden house and your lodgers this is turning out to be one heck of a day."

Odelia frowned. "Does this have anything to do with the spa you're building?"

Marge laughed. "Spa? What are you talking about? We're building a second bathroom." And when Odelia simply stared at her in wordless surprise, she continued, "With your grandmother hogging the bathroom every morning we had to do something. So we decided to turn the garden house into a bathroom. Only now Tex has gone and demolished it, figuring it wasn't sturdy enough. I just hope he'll be able to build that bathroom. Which reminds me—when Chase comes in, can you ask him if he's got a couple of hours to spare this weekend?"

"Sure thing, Mom," said Odelia, and yawned cavernously.

"Go and lie down," said Marge encouragingly. "You need it. Or better yet, come and crash at our place. With these Boggles you won't get a wink of sleep."

And so three generations of Poole women walked out of the house, and then it was just us… and those fearful Boggles! Which is why we quickly followed suit.

"A new bathroom?" said Harriet as we emerged through the pet flap. "I thought Gran said they're building a spa resort?"

"You need plenty of bathrooms in those resorts," said Brutus. "To wash off the mud from those mud baths and the sweat from those saunas. I'll bet this is just the first of many more." He shrugged. "You have to start somewhere."

It sounded reasonable enough, and since we were all pretty tired from the emotional rollercoaster we'd been through, we followed Odelia and Marge through the opening in the hedge, into the house, up the stairs, into Gran's room, where we all settled ourselves on the old lady's bed and were soon fast asleep.

CHAPTER 13

$\mathcal{A}$t some point Odelia joined us, and I must say we spent a fair time taking a well-deserved nap... until a loud voice awoke us. It seemed to come from somewhere nearby, and even though I didn't immediately recognize the voice, it was clear that Odelia did, for she groaned and said, "Oh, God, not again."

It was, of course, one of the guests of her Airbnb, namely Janine Boggle, inquiring loudly where her landlady had gone off to or words to that effect.

Odelia walked out of the room on her tippy toes, careful not to disturb us, and moments later I could hear her converse with her esteemed guest on the landing.

"Oh, there you are."

"I was just—"

"I wanted to talk to you about meal arrangements."

"Yes?"

"Well, the thing is that both John and I are very particular where our meals are concerned. As it is, we're vegetarians, and also we don't do dairy or gluten or anything that contains glutamate. So what did you have in mind for dinner?"

"Um, well, I have to admit I haven't, um…"

"Cause I was thinking about something simple yet hearty. Like perhaps a vegetarian wellington? Or enchiladas? Or penne with avocado? Oh, you know what would be great? Butternut squash and sage risotto. What do you think?"

"That… sounds like a good idea."

"Great. That's settled then. What time can we expect to sit down for dinner?"

"Oh, you mean I'm the one who—"

"I was thinking six o'clock. John and I are very particular about mealtimes. We think it's important to train one's digestive system to adhere to a strict regimen. So let's settle on six o'clock, shall we? And let's do lunch at twelve sharp. We like a light lunch—something simple like bean and halloumi stew."

"Hallou—"

"And while we're on the subject, we always breakfast at nine. I was thinking carrot cake porridge for me and fried egg Florentine toasties for John—whole-grain only, of course, and preferably spelt, if you can get it, einkorn if not."

"Ein…"

"Thanks ever so much, Amelia."

"It's actually Ode—"

"And don't forget about those beddings. It's important that John gets a good night's sleep. He's a very important man with a lot of important things to do."

The creaking of the stairs told us Janine had delivered her list of demands and was exiting the scene. Moments later Odelia entered the bedroom, and wordlessly dropped down on the bed. She looked a little shell-shocked, I had to say. And she'd only been lying there for about five seconds when she bounced up again, muttering something about having to do some shopping. And then she was off.

"It sure isn't easy being in charge of an Airbnb," Brutus remarked.

"No, it's certainly a full-time job," I agreed.

"So if an Airbnb is a bed and breakfast in the air, why is it in our house?" asked Dooley.

"How can a bed and breakfast be in the air, Dooley?" said Harriet.

"I don't know. I just pictured it like a hotel floating in the sky."

We all smiled at the quaint image Dooley had pictured, but then reality sunk in again. "I don't like to say this, you guys," said Brutus, "but I'm afraid we're all going to have to start looking for a new home."

"I'm afraid you're right," I said.

"With Odelia's place infested with guests and dogs, and Marge and Tex turning their home into a spa resort, it's obvious we've outstayed our welcome here."

"I hate to agree with you, Brutus, but when you're right, you're right."

"But I don't want to go," said Dooley. "I like it here. It's our home."

"Not anymore, it's not," said Harriet sadly. "Now it's the Boggles' home."

We all took a moment to let that sink in. It was a sobering thought. Then Brutus said, "Let's not fret, my friends. We had a good run, but it was going to end sooner or later. So let's simply approach this situation in a rational way. I'll bet there are plenty of places we can go."

"We could go and live with Uncle Alec," I suggested. "Or Charlene."

We'd spent some time with Charlene Butterwick, Alec's girlfriend, and even though she's not used to hosting cats, she'd still welcomed us into her home and had done her utmost to provide us with everything a grown cat needs.

"I like Charlene," said Harriet. "Uncle Alec, too, but his place is a mess."

"Bachelors," Brutus grunted, as if he was an expert on the subject, which perhaps he was, since he'd briefly stayed with Uncle Alec, back when Chase was still living with Odelia's uncle.

"Okay, so Charlene it is," I said. "So when do you propose we move in with her?"

"The sooner the better," said Brutus. "It's obvious that this place is about to turn into a building site, which will make our lives a living hell, and Odelia's house is already a disaster zone."

"It is," I said sadly. "It really is."

Just then, as if to spur us into action, somewhere nearby Grace opened her pipes again, and was wailing away to her heart's content, possibly expressing an urgent desire to be fed, or else she'd managed to fill up her diaper once more.

"It's an odd thing about babies, isn't it, Max?" said Dooley. "Either they're eating, or they're pooping, or both. Isn't there anything else they can do?"

"You mean like tricks or something?" said Brutus with a grin. "Babies aren't circus artists, Dooley, didn't you know?"

"No, I mean, they have a very limited range, don't they?"

This made Brutus laugh even louder. "Limited range! Like second-rate actors!"

"So when are we making the move to Charlene's place?" asked Harriet, who was grooming her shiny white fur. "Or do you think we should give the Pooles another day to get their act together and remember that they have a responsibility toward their cats?"

"We could give them until tomorrow," I said.

"You mean like a multitatum?" asked Dooley.

"An ultimatum, yes. This whole business with the Boggles obviously took Odelia by surprise. She probably hadn't expected them to be so demanding."

"Paying guests are always demanding," said Harriet. "They expect the very best, and if they don't get it they will leave a scathing review on Welp."

"Yelp," I corrected her.

"That's what I said."

"I think Airbnb has its own review system. No Yelp involved."

"Okay, so let's give them until tomorrow," said Brutus. "But if things don't improve within the next twenty-four hours, we're out of here—agreed?"

"Agreed," I said, with a touch of reluctance, for I like the Pooles—they're our family. Then again, Charlene is also family, and she probably wouldn't dream of turning her home into an Airbnb or a spa resort.

"I like Charlene," said Harriet. "She's very classy, like me."

"I also agree," said Dooley, "but only if I can watch the Discovery Channel in Charlene's place. Do you think she has a TV? I don't remember."

"Of course she has a TV," said Harriet. "I'll bet she has the latest model."

"I don't mind if it's not the latest model," said Dooley. "As long as it has the Discovery Channel." He sighed deeply. "I'll miss watching soaps with Gran."

"I'll miss a lot of things," I said.

"Let's not get mopey," said Brutus. "We'll still see the Pooles all the time. They can always come and visit." He got up and stretched. "I don't know about you, but I'm starving and I'm going to see if I can get a bite to eat."

And since the mention of food made my stomach rumble, I also got up, and in short order the four of us made our way downstairs and into the kitchen for a refreshing meal... until we saw that our bowls were completely devoid of kibble!

"Who did this!" Brutus cried, then directed his nose to the floor and sniffed. When he looked up again, there was a dangerous gleam in his eyes. "The Boggles," he growled. "It's those darn dogs again! They ate all of our food!"

And before we could stop him, he was off in search of the offending canines.

CHAPTER 14

*C*hase had had a rough day. A man had been found stabbed to death, another shot to death, and a third bludgeoned to death, and even though he wasn't supposed to lead investigations but be the guy steering his detectives from behind his desk, he'd still been compelled to go out into the field—literally, in this case—and do his bit for the good of the investigation. And so when he arrived home he was happy to sink down onto the couch and chill for a few minutes… until he discovered that two dogs had taken over his favorite couch!

"Odelia!" he cried. "What are these dogs doing here?!"

When no response came, he frowned and went in search of his wife. What he found instead was a large male with butter-colored floppy hair who looked like a clown. He was grinning at him, and as he extended his hand, said, "John Boggles, and you must be Mr. Poole."

Chase stared at the man, and wondered if he'd walked into the wrong house. "The name is Kingsley, actually. Chase Kingsley. May I ask—"

"I wanted to thank you personally, Mr. Kingsley, for the

hospitality you have shown me and my wife. Bravo, sir. Bravo." And he started a sort of earnest slow clap that made Chase look around in search of Ashton Kutcher and his hidden camera. Was this some kind of practical joke? Was his father-in-law behind this?

A woman now descended from the stairs who wasn't Odelia. She resembled a horse for some reason, and extended a frosty look at Chase.

"Darling, meet Chase Kingsley. Mr. Kingsley is Odelia's husband."

"Just the person I was hoping to see," said the woman, displaying rows and rows of teeth. "I don't know if your wife informed you that John has a bad back?"

"Threw it out in a game of cricket last fall," said Mr. Boggle. "Sticky wicket."

"At any rate, that bed simply won't do. It sags in the middle. One night on that bed and Johnny will need surgery."

"I don't like surgery," said the woman's husband. "I hate being put to sleep."

"So please arrange for a decent box spring, will you? Top of the line, please."

"Good mattress makes all the difference," Boggle confirmed. "Night and day."

"And please be quick about it," said the lady. "I want that mattress by tonight."

"How about you, my blossom?" asked Mr. Boggle.

"I'll survive," said the woman with a grim look on her face. It made her look like a horse that lost the derby. "Though I'd appreciate it if you'd find a decent mattress for me as well. It doesn't have to be as expensive as Johnny's, but it does have to support my back in all the right places. Sleep is important, Mr. Pringles."

"Kingsley," Boggle supplied helpfully.

"Right. Well, that'll be all for now," she said, and directed a scathing look at the two dogs. "That won't do," she muttered, and stalked over there to rearrange their blanket, which had become crumpled. But then Chase saw that it was actually Max and Dooley's favorite blanket, and he wondered if he'd suddenly entered the Twilight Zone, and Odelia had been replaced by this strange demanding woman, and Max and Dooley by these two dogs. But if that was so, who was Boggle?

"Prime Minister of England," said the man as if he'd read his mind. "Taking a holiday in Bumpkin Cove, your bucolic little town. Lying low, so to speak."

"You're... Prime Minister of England?" asked Chase. Curiouser and curiouser.

"Guilty as charged. Been the top man for years now, and I'm afraid people are starting to get bored with me. You know how it is. One moment you're more popular than Harry Styles, the next they're sick of you. Can't stand your face. Just the way these things go. Even Churchill lost his first election after the war." His face crumpled. "Though that thing with Janine didn't help matters, of course."

"Janine?"

"My wife," he said, gesturing to the horse-faced woman. "She insisted on giving 10 Downing Street a major overhaul, you see. Figured the previous chappies had despicable taste, and the thing needed sprucing up a goodish bit. I gave her free rein, of course, and I have to say she did a smashing job. Absolutely topping. Only it cost rather a good deal of doubloons, I'm afraid, and when the papers started throwing exorbitant sums around, it rather sunk my popularity. Which is why it was decided I needed to go into hiding for a while in the arse end of nowhere where those johnnies of the press would never find me." He slapped Chase on the back in a jovial manner. "Which is how we ended up here in Bumpkin Cove!"

Chase would have said something, but at that moment the pet flap flapped and four cats came racing in and made a beeline for the dogs ensconced on the couch. And the next few minutes were taken up by a sort of catfight, or cat-slash-dog fight, for there was a lot of hissing and a lot of barking, and Janine Boggle, if that was the woman's name, did a lot of hysterical screaming, furiously trying to extricate her dogs from the mêlée.

"Oh, my," said Mr. Boggle, rocking back and forth on his heels. "Rather reminds me of a sitting of the House of Commons."

CHAPTER 15

I could have said that the contretemps with Little John and Little Janine ended in a resounding victory for Brutus but I would be lying. Then again, it wasn't as if the fight proceeded entirely fair and square. As it was, Janine intervened by expertly yanking her dogs from the tussle and pressing them to her bosom in an attempt to vouchsafe them from being filleted by a justifiably outraged Brutus.

Even now, half an hour later, our friend was still licking his proverbial wounds.

"It's not fair," he was saying as we convened in the back-yard. "And Chase just standing there like a big doofus didn't help."

"He should have taken your side, sweet pea," said Harriet.

"He's our human, isn't he? Then why did he choose *their* side?!"

"To be fair, Chase didn't pick any side," I said. "He decided to stay neutral."

"Well, I think it's perfectly horrid of him," said Harriet. "Brutus is his cat."

"Technically…"

"Shut up, Max," said Harriet. "Whose side are you on, anyway?"

"Do we have to pick sides?" asked Dooley. "Can't we all live together in perfect harmony?"

"No, we cannot!" Harriet snapped. "And if you don't understand that, you have no right to call yourself a feline."

"But I don't call myself a feline. I call myself Dooley."

"There, there, poor baby," said Harriet, giving her mate a loving nudge.

But Brutus wasn't to be consoled. "I know we said we'd give the Pooles twenty-four hours to clean up their act, but now I'm not so sure. It's obvious they have picked their side, and it's not our side."

And as Brutus nursed his wounded pride and Harriet tried to patch up his damaged ego, Dooley and I decided to remove ourselves from the conversation for a little while. Since no food seemed forthcoming, either from Marge (busy with Grace) or Odelia (shopping for the Boggles) or Gran (building Poole Spa & Pool) and we had developed quite an appetite at this point (amazing how invigorating an old-fashioned dog fight can be) we thought we'd try our luck elsewhere.

As we were walking along the street, neatly keeping to the sidewalk as befitting a couple of pedestrians such as ourselves, Dooley said, "We should have known that the arrival of the baby would change everything, Max."

"You can't blame the Boggles on Grace, Dooley."

"But I do! If Grace hadn't arrived, Odelia would still be working as a reporter, and she would be far too busy to open a bed and breakfast in the sky."

"I'm sure the air in Airbnb doesn't actually refer to the sky, Dooley," I reiterated a point we'd discussed before.

"And if Grace hadn't come into our lives Marge and Tex

and Gran wouldn't be so desperate to make money that they're going to turn our home into a resort."

Which actually made me wonder how they were going to accomplish such a feat. As far as I know—and I know I'm not an expert by any stretch of the imagination—these resorts need a lot of space, especially when they're going to add in a hotel and all the necessary amenities your spa-going person likes to see.

"Look, Grace is here to stay, Dooley, and frankly I think adding a baby to the mix certainly has its benefits."

"Like what?" asked Dooley as we neatly sidestepped a sizable sampling of dog excrement that some overzealous canine had left behind and their human had failed to remove.

"Like… well… um… Oh, I have it. Odelia looks a lot happier, doesn't she?"

"She looks like a zombie, Max, and so does Chase."

"Well, yes, but underneath that tiredness I'm sure they're both very happy."

"They don't look happy. They look like they haven't slept in weeks."

Probably they hadn't, that much was true.

"Okay, so these first couple of weeks and months are tough, but when Grace starts sleeping through the night, I'm sure their lives will be much enriched."

"I've heard that's when the trouble starts," said my friend, who'd suddenly morphed into a sort of prophet of doom and gloom. "When they start to walk. That's when you have to watch out. They will escape any chance they get, and you have to watch them like a hawk. And then when they start teething it's even worse. You've got a standing appointment with the pediatrician, and then later, when they enter their teens you've got a standing appointment with a shrink. All in all, Max, I think kids should come with a health warning, just like cigarettes."

"I think you're looking at this all wrong, Dooley. Kids are fun! Kids are a source of great joy and happiness! Okay, so it's not always easy, but generally humans seem to enjoy having kids."

"They enjoy making kids, not having them."

I stared at my friend. "Who told you that?"

He looked bashful for a moment. "I overheard Gran tell her friend Scarlett once. Though I don't actually know what it means. It does sound nice, doesn't it?"

"It certainly sounds like something Gran would say," I agreed. "Look, Dooley. Babies aren't like a pair of shoes you buy online: you can't return them to sender. So we just have to accept that she's here and decide to make the best of things."

He sighed deeply. "I just hope Charlene won't have a baby with Uncle Alec."

It was a point I hadn't yet given any thought to. "How old is Charlene?" I asked.

"Isn't she the same age as Marge and Tex?"

I nodded thoughtfully. "Forty-eight. It's possible, I guess, though unlikely."

"You mean her clock is broken?"

"Her clock? What clock?"

"Odelia once told her mom that she heard her clock ticking and that's how she knew she had to have a baby. I asked her what clock this was, cause I couldn't see a clock, but she just laughed and patted me on the head."

"I think she was referring to her biological clock, Dooley."

"So where does she keep this biological clock? And how come no one else can hear it ticking?"

"Um…" Lucky for me we'd arrived in town, and the hustle and bustle of traffic distracted my friend to some extent. Soon we arrived at the General Store, where Kingman holds forth. Kingman belongs to Wilbur Vickery, who owns the General Store, and is a dear, dear friend of ours. He's very large and very chatty and is the cat to go to when you're dealing with an issue, great or small, since he knows all, or at least he thinks he does and so does everyone else in town, including me.

"Hiya, fellas," he said when he saw us approach, deftly avoiding being trampled on by passersby and his human's customers. "How are things?"

"Things are… interesting," I said.

"We're moving out," Dooley announced without preamble. "We're going to live with Charlene Butterwick from now on."

Kingman's eyebrows shot up. "Moving out? But why?"

"Odelia had a baby and also, she has started a bed and breakfast in the sky," Dooley explained, "and so she doesn't have time for us anymore. And Marge and Tex are opening a wellness resort and are going to turn their house into a hotel, their backyard into a pool and their garden house into a spa. So they won't have time for us anymore either."

"I'm sure you're exaggerating," said Kingman with a frown of concern.

"No, we're not," said Dooley. "They gave all of our food to the dogs, and we haven't had anything to eat since last night."

"Oh, you poor dears!" Kingman exclaimed. "Here, tuck right in!" He was pointing to a large bowl, filled to the brim with the good stuff. Kingman's human gets his kibble delivered in bulk, you see, and always has plenty to spare.

We didn't need to be told twice, and soon were snacking away to our heart's content. I have to say it hit the spot, and before long we'd managed to empty the bowl. On top of that an old lady who saw us digging in like a couple of famished scavengers took pity on our plight, and opened a can of sardines she'd bought. Now Odelia has often told us not to accept candy from strangers, but A) sardines aren't candy and B) we really were pretty starved at that point.

"So tell me all about what's going on," said Kingman once we'd finished our meal. "Odelia is starting a bed and breakfast?"

I nodded, licking my lips for those precious last crumbs. "Her first guests are a couple named the Boggles. He's a Prime Minister in England, apparently."

"And they have two horrible dogs who eat our food, sleep on our blanket, and treat us like surfers," Dooley supplied.

"I think Dooley means servants," I clarified.

"I've heard of this Boggle character," said Kingman. "Isn't he involved in some kind of scandal?"

"Possibly," I admitted.

"I saw something about him being removed from office for some reason."

"Removed from office? You mean he's not the Prime Minister anymore?"

"No, I don't think so. I didn't pay a lot of attention, but I seem to remember he took a trip to some private island resort belonging to some billionaire and forgot to declare it as an expense and some people got very upset—possibly his accountant or his taxman or both. At any rate, they replaced him with some other dude or dudette. Plenty of staff turnover in those top jobs, apparently. Not like with our president, who usually manages to stick around for the full four years."

I can tell you that this news wasn't received with perfect equanimity. Dooley and I shared a look of dismay.

"Max!" Dooley cried. "If Mr. Boggle is out of a job, that means he's never going to leave! He'll stay with us forever and ever and ever!"

CHAPTER 16

Odelia arrived back at the house with bags full of purchased goods, and had been thinking about the menu Janine had said she and John wanted to adhere to. She wondered how she was ever going to be able to please the demanding couple since she wasn't exactly a Julia Child or Martha Stewart in the kitchen. She staggered in with the bags, and hoped her mom and Grace were all right. She hated to impose on her mother, but the arrival of the Boggles was an emergency, and she couldn't very well let Tessa's good friends down in their hour of need.

The first person she met was Chase, who was talking on the phone and staring out of the window into the backyard. He turned when she entered and immediately jumped to her assistance by taking over one of the heavy bags.

"Yes, to be delivered immediately. Oh, and about that mattress, are you sure it's designed for people with a back injury? That's a great relief. Thank you."

She started putting away the groceries, and wondering if Chase had lost his job at the police station and had gone into the mattress business instead. After he'd disconnected, he joined her and said in a low voice, "What's the deal with these Boggles? I arrived home and suddenly there they were —and two dogs, too."

"I wanted to tell you but didn't want to trouble you when you were in the middle of your investigation," she said. "Tessa Torrance called and asked if we could help out some good friends of hers and Prince Dante's. John Boggle is in some kind of trouble at home and needs to disappear from the public eye for a while, and she thought the last place the media would look for him is here."

"Oh, so this was Tessa's idea, was it?" said Chase, and she had the impression he wasn't entirely happy with the state of affairs. "The cats and the Boggle dogs got into a fight," he added when she gave him a questioning look. "I think the dogs won, but I'm not an expert. The cats disappeared and I haven't seen them since."

"Oh, dear," said Odelia, and for the first time that day glanced down at her cats' bowls. They were all empty. "Oh, dear, oh, dear." Then she glimpsed into their litter boxes, and found that they were full... and smelly. And as far as she could tell, that was dog poo and not cat poo in there. "Oh, dear, oh, dear, oh, dear." No wonder the cats weren't happy.

"What's all this?" asked Chase, referring to the bags and bags of food.

"John Boggle has to stick to a very strict vegetarian diet, so Janine gave me some tips on what to cook for them."

The corners of Chase's mouth sagged. "Where is Grace?"

"Next door with my mother. I asked her if she could take care of her while I went shopping for the Boggles."

"Mh," said Chase with a frown. "They had me shopping, too. I just ordered a box spring for John, who apparently suffers from a bad back, and a new mattress for Janine as well. Which had me wonder where they'll be sleeping tonight."

Odelia gave him a sheepish look. "I asked my dad to help me bring down the old bed from the attic and I put them in the nursery. We're not using it anyway." Which was true, since Grace had been sleeping in the bedroom ever since they got back from the hospital. She lifted one of the bags from the counter.

"Honey, you really shouldn't be carrying these heavy bags," said Chase as he immediately took the bag from her. "You should be resting. Taking it easy."

"I know, but the Boggles—"

"Let me take care of the Boggles, all right?"

"But you have your big case to deal with."

"I know," he said, and drove his fingers through his dark mane. "But maybe I can talk to your uncle and he can take over for me."

"Out of the question. You can't ask Uncle Alec to take over for you so you can take over for me. That's just silly. No, I'll just…"

"You'll just what?"

She held up her hands. "I don't know. I guess I could ask… Gran?"

Chase lifted one sardonic eyebrow. "If you want to get rid of the Boggles, by all means ask your Gran to jump in."

"Yeah, probably not a good idea. So maybe…" Her mom already helped out with Grace, and between the library and this bathroom project, she'd have her hands full as well. She slumped a little. "I don't know, Chase. I really don't know what to do."

"We'll figure it out," he promised, and held her close and kissed the top of her head. "I don't know how, but we'll figure it out."

And that's how the Boggles, John and Janine, found them. "I say," said John, "I was going to take a shower but I seem to have some trouble getting the water really, really hot, you know. I like it hot—scalding, almost. Could you perhaps…"

Chase nodded. "It's an old system and needs careful handling." And both men left to deal with this hot shower emergency.

"I'm in something of a pickle myself," said Janine. "I don't seem to have quite the closet space I need. You wouldn't happen to have some extra space in your room, would you?"

"Of course," said Odelia, and pushed herself away from the counter. "I'll free up some space in our closet." And so she found herself reorganizing her closets so she could accommodate their guests. Janine had lots of gorgeous dresses, and it took a while to get them all on hangers. For the time being she removed her own dresses and Chase's suits, and piled them up in a corner of the room.

"If I could give you some advice?" said Janine, eyeing the bedroom with a critical eye. "I think you could work wonders with this space—absolute wonders. If you want I could give you some pointers. I'm an avid interior decorator and doing a home makeover is something of a passion of mine. I love a challenge."

She followed Janine's gaze and saw she was staring at a picture of Odelia and Grace. The picture was taken at the hospital, and Odelia thought she looked terrible, but Chase said it was his favorite picture of her and he just loved it.

"Do you have kids?" Odelia asked.

"No, I haven't," said Janine with a touch of wistfulness. "Though I want to."

"It's not too late. How old are you?"

"Thirty-eight."

"Plenty of time left," said Odelia with a smile.

"I know, but John…" Janine hesitated, then glanced in the direction of the door and lowered her voice. "John already has kids from a previous marriage, and he's not looking to have more. Though now I'm starting to regret having said I didn't want any either."

"Have you had that conversation?"

"Not really. John's been so busy these last couple of years…"

"Looks like he's less busy now," said Odelia. "So maybe now's the time to talk?" She gave the woman an encouraging smile. "Strike while the iron is hot, right?"

Janine gave her a lopsided grin. "Yes, I guess you're right."

Just then, Janine's dogs came tripping into the bedroom, took one look around, seemed to roll their eyes and walked right out again. Seen and disapproved.

CHAPTER 17

"Max?"

"Mh?"

"What if Charlene doesn't want us?"

"We don't know that, Dooley."

"No, but suppose she doesn't even like cats and is afraid to say?"

"What are you talking about?"

"Well, some people will say anything to please other people, especially when they're related to the man they love, in this case Uncle Alec. So maybe Charlene has been tolerating us all this time, but secretly hates cats from the bottom of her heart and when we go and live with her she'll do what she can to get rid of us."

"I think if Charlene was secretly a cat hater we would have noticed by now."

"But she's a politician, Max."

"So?"

"Politicians are trained to lie. They're the best liars on the planet. They're professionals. So she could lie to your face and you wouldn't even know it."

He had a point, of course. It is true that politicians, before they join the trade, go to politician school, where one of the main courses is 'lying for fun and profit.' The same thing goes for lawyers, bankers and hedge fund managers, who take some of the same courses.

"So… how do we find out, Max?"

"I guess we'll know soon enough," I said.

He gave me a look of concern. "What if she sneaks up on us in the middle of the night with a big butcher's knife and chops us up into little pieces? Or what if she makes a deal with a local butcher to sell us as meat and turn us into sausages?"

"Then I guess we'll have to be on our guard, Dooley."

"We'll take turns keeping watch," he said determinedly. "I'll take the first watch, and then you and Brutus and Harriet can take the next shifts. We can't allow her to get rid of us, Max. She's our last hope."

We were passing by one of those blind alleys, of which there are quite a few in Hampton Cove, and a loud voice hailed us. "Max! Dooley! Over here!"

I recognized the voice as belonging to our friend Clarice, whose favorite hobby is dumpster-diving. She's one of those free spirits, you see, and likes to live life on her own terms, untethered and unbound by the rules of society.

"Hey, Clarice," I said as we joined her underneath a sizable dumpster. She was snacking on some carrion, presumably the mortal remains of a rat. I shivered a little, and had to look away as she dug in with distinct relish.

"Long time no see," said Clarice, her keen eyes taking us in. She's a smallish cat, but tough as nails, with chunks missing from both ears and looking as if she's been through the wars, which presumably she has—a veteran of many a battle. She now narrowed her eyes at Dooley. "You look like you got something on your mind, Dooley. What's wrong?"

"Oh, Clarice, everything is wrong!" said Dooley with a catch in his voice.

"Oh, my," said Clarice. "You better tell me all about it."

"Odelia is starting a bed and breakfast in the sky, only she's not doing it in the sky but in our own home, and she's hosting the Prime Minister of England who's not the Prime Minister of England anymore because he was on a billionaire island and he forgot to tell people about it. And now his dogs are eating our food and sleeping on our blanket and they've taken over the house! And Tex is building a spa and is turning his house into a hotel and so we'll have to move out but Charlene hates cats but nobody knows because she's a politician and she took a lying course and she's going to murder us in our sleep and turn us into sausages!"

"Oh, dear," said Clarice with uncharacteristic softness.

"And now we don't know what to do!" Dooley finished his long lament.

"I see," said Clarice, then turned to me for clarification.

"It's true," I said. "More or less. I don't know about the sausage part, though."

"It could be hamburger patties," Dooley said with a sniffle.

"So looks like you guys are in a pickle, huh?" said Clarice, summing things up nicely. "And you're looking for a place to stay?"

We both nodded intently. "A place where they won't try to kill us or kick us out or both," Dooley added. It's a stipulation I think all pets would agree with.

"This is one of those moments where the appropriate response would be 'I told you so,'" said Clarice. "But since I'm a nice kitty I won't gloat." She was smirking a little, though, but with Clarice it's hard to tell, since she has so many scars it's tough to read her expression. "Don't place your trust in humans, fellas!" she said emphatically. "It only leads to disappointment and heartbreak. You have to learn to take care of yourself. I mean, look at me. I'm perfectly happy. I do what I want, when I want—got plenty of chow, lots of friends—I'm living the perfect life! So instead of whining and moping, rejoice! You're finally free! Free of the tethers of those terrible restrictions a life in the lap of luxury invariably brings!"

We both stared at her, not fully comprehending what she was saying. "So your point is…" I said.

"You don't need Odelia or Marge or Vesta or any of these utterly unreliable humans. These streets are your home! In other words: the world is your oyster!"

"I don't like oysters," said Dooley.

"Me, neither," I said. "Too slimy for my taste."

Apparently this wasn't the right answer, for Clarice grumbled something under her breath, then tore another piece off the carcass lying between her paws.

"You don't understand, Clarice," I said. "We're not like you. We haven't lived on the streets all our lives. We're creatures of comfort, used to a lovely home, a warm body to cuddle up to, our bowls always filled with our favorite kibble…"

"In other words: spoiled rotten."

"Yes, yes, all right, I admit it: we're spoiled. Which is why I think it would be hard for us to adjust to life on the street. I mean, it's all fine and dandy in the summer, when the weather is nice and you can sleep under a tree. But in wintertime, when it's freezing and snowing, it's going to be tough!"

"Brrrr," said Dooley, shivering. "I don't like snow. It's very cold and very wet."

"Pussies," Clarice growled, shaking her head in disgust. "I should have known my good advice would be wasted on you."

"It's not wasted," I assured her. "In fact we might take you up on it. If Charlene turns out to be a secret cat hater, we won't have any other recourse but to adjust to life on the street."

"We could always go and live with Wilbur and Kingman," Dooley suggested.

"I don't think Wilbur would agree to take in another four cats," I said.

"Oh, you bunch of crybabies," Clarice growled. "Look around! There's plenty of people who'll take you. In fact the world is filled with people who want nothing more than to coddle and spoil you rotten. Just put an ad in the paper—or better yet, post something on Facebook and you'll have people clamoring to adopt you."

"You think?" said Dooley, blinking excitedly. "That's great news, Clarice!"

"Get out of here," said Clarice with a throwaway gesture of her paw. "You guys make me sick. Just get lost already. Go on, get!"

"But Clarice," said Dooley. "You have to tell us more about these Facebook people."

"For crying out loud," she grumbled, stalking off in the direction of the next dumpster. "Talk about a couple of namby-pamby cats wasting my precious time."

"Well, I guess we'll see you later, Clarice," I said.

But she'd already jumped into the dumpster, and judging from the sounds of a feverish scuffle, was probably in the process of catching herself another juicy rat.

"Thanks for the advice, Clarice!" Dooley shouted, and then we were on our way again. "We have to do this, Max," he said as we wended our way home again. "We have to put a post on Facebook, saying we're looking for a new home."

"Let's do that first chance we get," I agreed.

"Harriet will know what to do. She's a social media

maven. If Clarice is right, we'll have a new home in no time. And maybe this one won't be as noisy and polluted with annoying guests as the last."

And on this hopeful note, we commenced our trek back.

CHAPTER 18

*V*esta stood looking at the remnants of the garden house with a big frown on her face. "Before you knocked down this thing you could have thought about removing my gardening tools first," she said.

"I know. I didn't think," said her son-in-law as he gave her a rueful look.

"It's fine. The lawnmower took a hit but he's a sturdy old sucker so he'll live. Now we need to get going on that wall over there. I suggest you take out the center piece first, then gradually work your way to Ted and Marcie's hedge."

"I'm not taking out that wall. Are you crazy? Blake Carrington will sue me."

"No, he won't. I told you, Blake will only be too happy that finally this worthless piece of land is going to be put to good use. And you can split the proceeds of the spa once things get going well. And trust me: people are gonna come from all over town to take a dip in the Poole pool." She grinned. "Thought of that myself."

"Vesta—"

"We've got a gold mine here, Tex, so let's cut the chitchat and get cracking."

But instead of putting his sledgehammer to good use, Tex crossed his arms in front of his chest and gave her a mutinous look. It was a look she was accustomed to.

"What is it now?" she said, trying to dredge up some much-needed patience from the depths of her being. She'd known from the start that living with Tex Poole wouldn't be easy, and she'd resigned herself to always be kind and take his weird quirks and peccadillos in stride, like a good mother-in-law must. She didn't suffer fools gladly but this was one fool she had to tolerate, for Marge's sake. But if he was going to stand in the way of progress, he had another thing coming.

"I'm not building a spa, Vesta. I'm building a second bathroom."

"Oh, not again with the bathroom, Tex. You're starting to sound like a broken record. Just put your back into it and get smashing. Just imagine you're the Incredible Hulk or something. Hulk smash!"

But Tex wasn't budging. So Vesta did the only sensible thing: she took a firm hold of that sledgehammer and dragged it over to the separating wall.

"Do I have to do everything myself?" she grumbled as she tried to lift the thing. It was a lot heavier than she thought, and the moment she'd managed to hold it over her head, she toppled backward and fell on her tush. "Darn it."

"I don't know why you insist on building a spa," said Tex, helping her to her feet. "We don't have the space or the permission, and we certainly don't have the expertise to build or run a spa. Nor do I want to run a spa, and neither does Marge."

"Well, I want to run a spa," said Vesta stubbornly. "There's a lot of money in wellness, Tex, or haven't you noticed?"

"Oh, I've noticed, all right, but it's not a business I want to get into. I'm a doctor, and Marge is a librarian, and we're both perfectly happy doing what we do."

"Okay, fine. So I'll build the spa, and I'll run it all by my lonesome."

"You can't build and run a spa, Vesta."

"Watch me," she said, and spat on her hands and grabbed the sledgehammer again. No one could ever accuse her of giving up at the first hurdle. She was a go-getter, a doer, a woman of action! She could teach Wonder Woman a thing or two!

"For God's sakes, give me that hammer before you hurt yourself." He took hold of the hammer and tried to drag it from her hands.

"Let go!" she said. "It's my hammer!"

"No, it's not. Just give it to me!"

"No way! I'm building myself a spa even if it kills me!"

"If you keep this up you just might get your wish. Now give!"

"Never!"

The tug of war continued unabated for the next few moments, until finally Vesta had enough and let go. The upshot was that Tex staggered back, lost his grip on the hammer, which swung up and described a perfect arc through the air and finally landed in their next-door neighbors' backyard.

There was a crashing sound, and Vesta and Tex shared a look of consternation, then both ran in the direction the heavy hammer had landed. And as they glanced across the hedge, they saw that the tool had smashed straight into a large garden gnome—the pride of Ted Trapper's collection. The business end of the sledgehammer had taken out the head of the gnome, which now had to go through life without a head. No great loss, but Ted might think different.

"Maybe we can glue it back together?" Vesta suggested.

"It looks pretty smashed up," said Tex.

"Yeah, it looks… pulverized."

Tex let out an involuntary chuckle, which caused Vesta to release a high-pitched giggle, and soon they were both shaking with mischievous mirth.

"We better remove that hammer before Ted finds out," said Tex finally.

"Give me a leg up," Vesta suggested. "I'll go and get it."

"Are you sure?"

"Yeah, just do it."

So Tex gave her a leg up, and Vesta clambered across that hedge, looking in the direction of the house to make sure Ted or Marcie hadn't noticed, grabbed the hammer and dragged it back to the hedge, then lifted it with some effort—the thing was hea-*vy*!

"Got it," said Tex, then helped her back to the other side.

She held up her hand and he clapped it in a perfect high five.

"Well done, pardner," she said.

"Well done yourself," he said.

"Too bad about that gnome."

He shrugged. "Oh, well."

It wasn't a big secret that Tex had never liked the fact that Ted had started his own gnome collection after Tex had started his, and that a healthy rivalry had soon developed between the two neighbors over who possessed the nicest and most expensive collection of gnomes. Looked like Ted was now one gnome down. And Tex certainly wouldn't shed any tears—quite the contrary, in fact.

"So about that spa," she began as they walked back to the house.

"Oh, God, will you cut it out with the spa already!" he cried.

"But it's such a great concept!"

"I don't care!"

"But, Tex!"

"No means no!"

"Maybe a small spa? Like a mini-spa?"

"No!"

"You won't even notice. I'll keep it really tiny. A teeny-tiny spa."

"No!"

"You're so unreasonable!"

And so, as the poet said, the long day wore on.

CHAPTER 19

*M*arge eyed baby Grace with a benevolent eye. She loved babysitting her granddaughter. Granddaughter. Now wasn't that something? She had a granddaughter. Which meant she was now a grandmother, and Tex was a grandfather. My, my. Just then, Tex and Marge's mom came walking into the kitchen, both looking a little heated. Presumably they'd gotten into another argument about the so-called spa, even though there had never been any mention of a spa.

The moment their gaze fell upon the domestic scene of Marge feeding Grace a bottle of Odelia's self-made brew, their truculence immediately ceased and they both took a seat at the kitchen table.

"Isn't she just the cutest?" said Ma. "She gets that from my side of the family."

"I'm sure she gets that from my side of the family," Tex countered.

"How can you say that? She's the spitting image of my grandmother—may she rest in peace—who also had a little dimple in her cheek."

"Lots of babies have dimples in their cheeks, Ma," said Marge. "That doesn't mean anything."

"She's a Muffin," Ma insisted. "Of course she is. And I'll bet she can talk to cats, too, which will be the litmus test." She leaned forward and dabbed her finger against Grace's pink cheek. "Can you talk like a cat? Oh, yes, you can. Oh, yes, you can. Say something."

"Ma! Just leave her alone."

"Fine. But she's a Muffin."

"She is a little muffin, isn't she?" said Tex softly. He smiled at the baby. "Our granddaughter, honey. Can you believe it? We're grandparents now."

"I know," said Marge. "Isn't that something?"

"And I'm a great-grandmother," said Ma, though she didn't look entirely happy to make that discovery. "Great-grandma Muffin." She cocked her head. "Have to get used to that one."

"So when is my bathroom going to be finished?" Marge asked.

"Soon," Tex promised. "I talked to your brother and he and Chase will give me a hand this weekend. Together we should be able to put something together."

"Or not," said Ma.

"Have a little faith in your son-in-law, Ma," said Marge. "He knows what he's doing. Don't you, honey?"

"Absolutely," said Tex, though he didn't look entirely convinced.

"I still think you should give that spa idea another chance," said Ma.

"Oh, God," said Tex, sinking his head in his hands.

"No spa, Ma," said Marge. "We don't need it."

"I need it!"

"No, you don't. You've got a perfectly fine job at the office."

"Perfectly boring job, you mean," the old lady grumbled. "Having to listen to people whining about their kidney stones or blather on about their bladder."

"You're doing something good for mankind. It's a noble profession."

"Says you."

Marge sighed and decided not to get worked up. Bad vibes for Grace. "By the way, can you check next door when you have a moment, honey? I have a feeling Odelia is in over her head with those guests of hers."

"Guests? What guests?" said Tex, watching on in fascination as Grace wrapped her tiny little digits around his index finger.

"Oh, Tex. The guests! The Boggles!"

"What Boggles? What are you talking about?"

"John and Janine Boggle are staying next door. He's the Prime Minister of England and she's his wife. Apparently Tessa Torrance called and asked if they could stay over for a couple of days."

"The Prime Minister of England is staying next door?"

Marge bit back a groan of exasperation. She loved her husband dearly, but sometimes he seemed to live on a different planet than the rest of them. "Yes, he arrived this morning and is planning to stay for a while."

"But he shouldn't—he can't—Odelia has to rest."

"I know, which is why you better go and check on her. I already said I'd help with the cooking and the cleaning, and maybe you can also chip in."

"Doing what?"

"I don't know, Tex—anything!"

"Uh-huh," he said, looking unconvinced. "Does he have health issues? Is that why he's staying with our daughter?"

"I don't think so."

"He just got canned from his job as PM," said Ma, who

was gently tickling Grace's belly and receiving a lot of exuberant giggles as a reward.

"He got fired from his job?" asked Marge. This was news.

"Sure. Defrauded someone or something or whatever. I don't know. I just scanned the headlines. Politicians behaving badly doesn't make for interesting reading."

Tex, who'd been scrolling on his phone, said, "Looks like he accepted a trip to some tropical private island as a gift from a billionaire friend of his."

"So? What's wrong with that?" said Ma. "If I had a billion-aire friend and he offered me a trip to his private island I'd be on a plane quick as a flash."

"The Prime Minister of a nation can't accept free trips, Ma," said Marge. "It opens him up to all kinds of accusations of favoritism."

"I don't get it," said Ma with a frown. "Who doesn't like to be the favorite?"

"Okay, so what if this billionaire owns a chain of super-markets, and wants to build a superstore in the heart of London, only he's been having trouble getting permission, and now all of a sudden his plans are being fast-tracked. People will say that he bought the approval by bribing his good friend the PM."

"Okay. Still don't get it."

"It's called corruption, all right? Which is why politicians cannot accept gifts from anyone. And even if Boggle did nothing wrong, it still looks bad that he would be hobnob-bing with billionaires on their private island."

"I say live and let live, but that's just me," said Ma.

"If this guy is out of a job," said Tex. "Does that mean he's flying home soon? Or that he'll stick around indefinitely?"

They all shared a look of concern. "Go over there now, Tex," Marge insisted. "Your daughter needs you."

"Yes, Tex," said Ma with a slight grin. "For once in your

life be a man and do something." Once Tex was off, huffing a little and muttering something to himself, Marge gave her mother a look of disapproval, she added, "What? What did I say?"

Marge sighed and gently tapped her granddaughter's nose. "This is the family you've chosen, honey. Are you sure you want to stick around?"

"We're a good family," muttered Ma. "The best." Then she brightened. "So have you considered how much money a spa can—"

"No, Ma. No spa."

"But—"

"No spa!"

"Oh, fine. Don't get your knickers in a twist, will you?"

Just then, Grace gurgled something and pulled Ma's nose.

"Who needs a spa when we've got you, mh?" said Marge.

"You're right," said Ma. "Who needs a spa anyway?"

Marge looked up sharply. "Did you just tell me I'm right?"

"I know," said Ma. "I must be softening with old age."

Or because she'd just become a great-grandmother.

"Not that I'm old, mind you. Older, yes, but still young."

"Of course, Ma. Of course."

CHAPTER 20

*S*ome kind of big to-do or hubbub was in progress when Dooley and I arrived at the house. On the way home we'd discussed the matter further and decided that if Charlene turned out to be a sausage-eating cat hater, we needed a plan B, and had landed on Gran's friend Scarlett as the next best option. Scarlett doesn't own pets, I know for a fact that she doesn't hate us, and she's very nice. And it's always better to pick a person you know than some unknown on Facebook.

So all in all we were feeling in an uplifted state of mind when we turned a corner and entered Harrington Street. We'd tell Odelia we were leaving tonight, and then first seek out Charlene, stay the night as a trial run, and then if things didn't work out, move in with Scarlett tomorrow. In other words, a foolproof plan.

Only when we had almost reached the house, we met with an unusual sight: Odelia was walking two dogs: Little John and Little Janine. Our human—or soon-to-be ex-human—looked dead on her feet, and I immediately felt sorry for her. And when we approached, she barely managed to give us a smile in greeting.

"Take us further afield, will you, Odelia?" said Little John. "I don't like these trees."

"Yes, take us to the dog park," Little Janine chimed in. "I've heard good things about the dog park. Not that I expect it to be up to our usual standards, but at least it's something."

"And better than these utterly useless trees and these tired old lampposts," her friend added.

"You don't like our trees?" I asked. "Or our lampposts?"

"No, we don't," said Little Janine with a tilt of the head.

"They smell funny," said Little John, making a face.

"I can tell that the dogs that use this street have absolutely no breeding."

"No breeding at all. Street mutts, one and all."

"In other words, common folk. Probably inbred, too."

The two dogs shared a smirk, then tugged at their respective leashes.

"To the dog park, please!" said Little John. "And be quick about it!"

"Yes, we haven't got all day!" Little Janine added.

"What do they want?" asked Odelia, not bothering to stifle a yawn.

"They want to go to the dog park," I said.

"They don't like our street," said Dooley.

"Too dirty and too common and populated with inbred mutts."

"Oh," said Odelia, then sighed. "Fine. I guess we're going to the dog park."

And since we needed to have a chat with her anyway, we decided to tag along.

"Is it true that your human was fired from his job?" asked Dooley, addressing Little Janine. "Only, a friend of ours told us about it, and now we were wondering if he's going to stay here or go back to England and look for another job?"

"Fired? Puh-lease," said Little Janine. "People like Big John don't get fired—they're the ones doing the firing."

"So you better watch out, little one," said Little John. "Or he'll fire you!"

They had a good laugh about that, even though I didn't think it was all that funny.

"They can't fire us," said Dooley, "cause we're leaving."

"Leaving?" said Little Janine. "What do you mean?"

"Oh, just let them," said Little John. "We're better off without them anyway."

"Yes, but who's going to make sure we get the right kind of food? And who's going to tell Odelia where to take us and when? We need them as translators."

"I'm not your translator," I said. "Where did you get that idea?"

"Oh, but you are," said Little Janine. "Of course you are. Didn't you know? You two work for us. And so does Odelia. In fact your whole family now works for us. Because Big John is Prime Minister, and that means he's in charge of everything."

"Just England," I pointed out. "Over here he's in charge of nothing at all."

"And since he was fired, he's not even in charge of his own country anymore," Dooley added.

This seemed to cause the twosome a measure of concern. But they quickly rallied. "Like I said, Big John doesn't get fired," Little Janine insisted. "He's the big honcho, and big honchos never get fired. Ever."

"What are you guys talking about?" asked Odelia with a tired smile.

"Oh, this and that," I said. She probably didn't need to

know that Big John's dogs considered her their personal slave. She had enough to deal with as it was.

We'd almost reached the park when we bumped into Kurt Mayfield, who was walking Fifi, and Ted Trapper, who was walking Rufus, his sheepdog. And even though the encounter was a pleasant one for the pet contingent, the humans were a lot less matey.

"Is it true that you are suing us because our daughter makes too much noise, Kurt?" asked Odelia, deciding to tackle this thing feet first. "Cause you should probably know that all babies are a little noisy. It's a natural thing. And if you sue us, not only does that make you a very petty person, but you're going to lose."

"Who told you that I'm suing you?" asked Kurt, already backtracking a little.

"I did," Fifi piped up happily from the man's feet, though of course he couldn't understand what she was saying.

"Just something that's being said around the neighborhood," said Odelia.

"Well done, Fifi," Rufus grunted. "About time someone said something about your human's appalling behavior."

"Would you call him appalling?" said Fifi, cocking her head.

"I'm not calling *him* appalling. I'm calling out his appalling behavior."

"Um… well… look," said Kurt. "I may have made an ill-advised remark at some point, or maybe someone misunderstood, but of course I didn't mean it. I mean…"

"Yes, Kurt," said Odelia. "What do you mean?"

"I, um… I don't have anything against infants, of course. And so what if I have to sleep with earplugs every night? I guess you and Chase have it a lot worse."

"It's true that we haven't been getting a lot of sleep lately," said Odelia, yawning.

"I hope you don't mind me saying so, Odelia, but you look terrible," said Ted.

"Thanks, Ted," said Odelia with a grimace. "That's very considerate of you."

"She does look terrible," said Little Janine. "Which makes me wonder if she's fit for her duties. Something to consider, Little John."

"Absolutely. Maybe Big John should look for a replacement."

"Oh, and now that I have you here," said Ted, "do you by any chance know who destroyed Big Papa?"

"Big Papa? Who's Big Papa?" asked Odelia.

"Big John, of course," said Little John. "He's like a father to his people."

"My gnome," said Ted. "When I went to pick up Rufus just now, I saw that Big Papa had lost his head."

"It happens," said Kurt sympathetically. "We all lose our heads from time to time. Just like I lost my head when little Grace arrived next door and started keeping me up at night." When Odelia shot a cross look in his direction, he held up his hands in a peaceable gesture and quickly added, "Which is absolutely understandable. She is, as you so rightly point out, just a baby. And babies cry. I accept that and I'm moving on."

"So about Big Papa," said Ted.

"I don't know anything about your gnome, Ted," said Odelia. "I'm sorry."

"I was thinking that maybe your dad… He was handling a sledgehammer earlier today, demolishing that eyesore of a garden house of his."

"Like I said, I don't know anything about any of that," said Odelia.

"Some babies do cry a lot louder than others, though," said Kurt. "Have you considered taking Grace to a doctor? Maybe there's something wrong with her."

The look Odelia shot him should have told him that he was treading on dangerous ground, but then Kurt has never been known for his sensitivity.

"It's just that he's my number-one gnome," said Ted. "The prize of my collection. Which is why he's called Big Papa. And now that he's lost his head it's just not the same. A papa without a head loses the respect of the other gnomes."

"Just glue his head back on, Ted," said Kurt gruffly.

"Well, I can't glue his head back on, Kurt, since his head has been pulverized," said Ted. "Literally turned to powder. Which means he must have suffered a heavy blow. Like from a sledgehammer," he added, giving Odelia a meaningful look.

"Maybe something fell from the sky?" Kurt suggested.

"Something fell from the sky," said Ted, with a voice dripping with skepticism.

"It happens. I read in the paper the other day that a frozen pizza fell on top of someone's head. Presumably dropped from an airplane."

"Oh, so one of the pilots decided they didn't like their Papa John's pepperoni order and opened a window on their jumbo jet and chucked it out, did they?"

Kurt's face flushed. "Are you calling me a liar, Ted?"

Ted immediately backed down. Accountants aren't big on fistfights with scrappy neighbors, even when they're fellow members of their local Homeowners Association. "I'm just saying it's very unlikely that pizzas fall from airplanes, Kurt. Nothing more. And besides, I didn't find any pizza anywhere near Big Papa."

"Look, you fellows can duke it out as much as you want," said Odelia, "but I have to take John Boggle's dogs to the dog park, so I bid you both adieu for now."

"John Boggle? *The* John Boggle?" said Ted, staring at the two dogs.

"The Prime Minister?" asked Kurt, his eyes also riveted on the dogs.

"That's the one." Though I could tell that Odelia already regretted having said anything. After all, the Boggles' stay with us was supposed to remain a secret.

"Only he's not the PM anymore, is he?" said Ted. "He got canned last week."

Odelia frowned. "John isn't Prime Minister of England anymore?"

"Nope," said Ted, looking pleased as punch that he knew something the others didn't—especially Kurt, who was giving him a distinctly dirty look. "Got sacked by his party for unethical behavior and replaced by another fellow—don't ask me who."

"Huh," said Odelia. "Is that a fact?"

Little John and Little Janine appeared taken aback by this confirmation from an unsuspected source that their unsackable human had, in fact, been sacked.

"Impossible," said Little John.

"Must be some mistake," said Little Janine.

"Big John would never allow himself to be fired."

"If you'll excuse me, I have somewhere I need to be," said Odelia, as she started in the direction of the homestead.

"Hey, what about the dog park!" Little Janine cried.

"Yes, I need to go—urgently!" Little John added.

"What can I say, you guys," I said. "You probably should have gone when you had the chance."

And then we were hurrying back to the house, Little John and Little Janine walking a little awkwardly, as they had a bladder control issue to contend with.

CHAPTER 21

*C*hase was helping the delivery guy wrestle the box
spring and the new mattress up the stairs and into
the nursery, which had temporarily morphed into a guest
room once again, also assisted by a large and burly male
he'd found standing in the living room and who had
announced he went by the name Wilkins and was John
Boggles's personal protection officer. The work was slow
going, as the staircase had never been designed to allow for
the transition of large objects like bulky box springs. Still,
while Wilkins pushed, and Chase pulled, and the delivery
guy was vocal in his helpful instructions, they were slowly
getting there.

Once upstairs, they found John Boggles in 'his' room
reading a Churchill biography and looking a little shaggy, as
was apparently his personal style. "Oh, there you are," he said
when they came a-knocking with the requested goods. "Just
put it... over there somewhere," he said, gesturing in the
general direction of the wall, where the butterflies Odelia
had painstakingly painted and the Smurfs Chase had cut out
and glued in place were still very much in evidence. Perhaps

one day, when these people had left, the room would be a nursery once again.

"So are you the English guy?" asked the delivery man, staring at John as if he was some kind of superhero in the flesh. "The one that got kicked out of office?"

"Um, yes, as a matter of fact I am he," said Boggles. "That is to say, he is I. I am him, so to speak. Though I think you'll find that I have not, as you so aptly put it, been 'kicked out of office,' but am in fact still very much in possession of my position."

The delivery guy, who'd been listening with rapt attention, seemed confused as to what Boggles had actually said, as evidenced by his next statement. "So are you moving into a Hollywood mansion now, like your Prince what's-his-face?"

"I can emphatically state that I am not moving into a Hollywood mansion," said Boggles. "I am merely enjoying the heartwarming hospitality of Mr. Pringsley here and his lovely wife Ophelia, and very soon I'll be back at my post, leading my country to infinity and beyond." He chuckled, then patted the man on the back. "Now if you could show me how to work this intriguing contraption of yours I'd be very much obliged, good sir."

Wilkins, who'd been standing at attention near the window, glancing out, now announced into a wrist mic, "All clear, I repeat, all clear, over."

Chase sidled up to the man. "So are there a lot of you guys out there, Wilkins?"

"I'm afraid I'm not at liberty to say, sir," said the security man stiffly.

"No, of course," he said. "It's just that you guys usually travel in packs, right?"

But Wilkins merely stared at him, then returned his gaze to the perimeter of the house, scanning it for known and unknown potential threats. Just then, Odelia moved into view, accompanied by two dogs and two cats. She waved at them and Chase waved back, while Wilkins muttered into his wrist mic, "F1 has returned with Boggle one and Boggle two, over."

"Her name is Odelia," said Chase helpfully. "And she's my wife."

"I know she's your wife, sir," said the man. "Now if you'll please let me do my job?"

"Oh, absolutely," said Chase, and decided to head down-stairs to greet his wife. As he did, he couldn't help but wonder how long these people were going to stay. He didn't mind that Odelia had decided to help out a friend, but the request had come at an inconvenient time, to say the least.

He met Odelia in the living room and saw that she looked perturbed. "What's wrong?" he asked as he watched the two dogs scoot through the pet flap and into the backyard, then make a beeline for the rose bushes for some reason.

"I met Kurt and Ted just now, and Ted says Boggles was fired from his job. He's no longer a Prime Minister, which makes me wonder what else he hasn't told us."

Chase frowned. "But... he just told us he's still the Prime Minister."

Odelia threw up her hands. "He's lying! It's all over the papers!"

"Calm down, honey," he said, placing his hands on her arms. "So what if he's not the Prime Minister anymore? What difference does it make?"

"The difference is that he might stick around here forever, Chase!"

He could see that she was a little—or a lot—overwrought, and it wasn't hard to understand why. Instead of enjoying those blessed postnatal weeks, she was running around doing the Boggles' shopping and playing the perfect hostess.

"So maybe we should find them some other place to stay?" he suggested gently. "I'll bet there's plenty of Airbnb's in town where they could stay."

"Tessa said they need to lay low for a while—to hide from the press."

"I'm sure that can be arranged in one of those nice Airbnb's. We could rent it under our own name, for instance, and nobody will be any the wiser."

She gave him a thoughtful look. "That's not such a bad idea, actually."

"We can discuss it over dinner," he said. "I'm making my signature dish, which I'm sure the Boggles will love, and we'll hear what they have to say."

"You're not making spaghetti bolognese?"

"Of course. Who doesn't love a nice bolognese?"

"But they're vegetarians."

He shrugged. "So I'll remove the meatballs."

"Did you manage to get the box spring and the mattress?"

"They're upstairs being installed as we speak."

"Oh, Chase, I'm so sorry for this mess. I shouldn't have said yes to Tessa."

"I'm sure it'll all work out fine," he assured her, and they shared a hug. Which is when he noticed that two cats were intently staring at him. "Honey?"

"Mh?"

"Have you fed the cats?"

"Oh, shoot," she said, disentangling herself from his embrace. "Completely forgot about that." She knelt down next to Max and Dooley. "You guys are probably starving. Let's get that fixed right now." She tickled them under the chin, which seemed to mollify them to some extent. She hurried into the kitchen, and he could hear her rummage around in the pantry, then utter a curse.

"What's wrong?" he said as he was starting to grow a little

uneasy under the cats' enduring stare—which could almost be qualified as a hostile glare at this point.

"We've run out of kibble! I gave the last portions to the Boggle dogs."

"That's all right. I'm sure your mom will have some."

"No, she ran out, too. Said she was going shopping tomorrow anyway."

"Didn't you go shopping this morning?"

Odelia reappeared, looking flustered. "I did, but Janine gave me such a long shopping list I completely forgot to buy kibble."

"We've got nothing left?" asked Chase, swallowing as Max and Dooley's stare turned lethal. "Not even some pouches of that nice, delicious wet food?"

"Nope. The Boggle dogs ate the lot. They might be tiny, but boy can they eat."

Just then, the cats broke out in some sort of remonstrative wailing, and Odelia looked startled.

"Oh, dear," she said.

"What are they saying?"

"This was the last straw. They're moving out and moving in with Charlene." She frowned as Dooley seemed to say something else. "At least if Charlene doesn't turn them into sausages. In which case they'll move in with Scarlett instead."

And to show them they weren't kidding, the two cats marched in the direction of the front door, which was still open, and strutted out and were gone.

CHAPTER 22

*W*e'd just left the house, making our big exit—though without slamming the door, since cats aren't into slamming doors—when a limousine came gliding along the street and pulled to a stop in front of us. A blacked-out window rolled down and the face of Tessa Torrance appeared. She removed her sunglasses, glanced down to me and Dooley and recognition registered on her refined features. "Look, Dante, isn't that Odelia's cat? That fat orange one?"

A second face joined the first, and I recognized Prince Dante. "I don't know, sugar plum. All cats look the same to me."

"I'm sure it's them," said Tessa, and called out to the driver. "Park over here, will you, George? Thanks." And she got out.

I would have told her I was neither fat nor orange but was distracted by her exquisitely fashionable appearance: she looked as if she was on her way to a *Vogue* shoot, in a black strapless dress and black lacquered heels. Dante, too, was dressed to impress in a charcoal tux.

"Are you sure this is the place?" the Prince asked.

"This is the address I've got." She directed her attention to me, giving me a thousand-watt smile. "Hey, cutie-pie, is this where Odelia Poole lives?"

"Odelia Kingsley," I said automatically. "And I'm not orange—I'm blorange."

"And he's not fat either," Dooley put in. "He's simply suffering from big bones."

"Not suffering, per se," I said. "Just one of those things one learns to live with."

"See?" said Tessa. "I told you I got it right the first time."

"How can you tell from a couple of meowing cats?"

"How many times do I have to tell you? Cats don't just meow—they talk."

They started up the short path to the front door. "So you can understand cats now?"

"Of course not, silly. Just trust me. When have I ever been wrong?"

And as they approached the house, Odelia appeared, looking distraught. Her first instinct was to bellow our names, and she'd just started, "Max, Doo—" when she caught sight of Tessa and Dante. "Oh…" she said, brought up short.

"Odelia!" Tessa cried, and opened her arms for a hug.

"Oh, Tessa," said Odelia, and suddenly burst into a flood of tears.

"What's wrong?" Tessa cried.

"Nothing—everything!"

And as the human contingent moved inside, Dooley and I shared a look of distress. "Suddenly I don't feel so good about moving in with Charlene, Max," said my friend.

"Me, neither."

"And it's not because she might have a sausage factory in her basement."

"I think it's doubtful that a mayor would also be a butcher on the side."

"We can't leave Odelia in her hour of need, Max. That woman needs us."

"She does. She really does."

"If we leave now, it's like kicking a dog. Even though I don't like most dogs—except Fifi and Rufus, of course—I would never kick them."

"Me, neither."

"Also because if I did they'd come after me."

"There's that, too," I allowed.

And so it was decided: we wouldn't leave Odelia when she was so obviously at a low ebb. Which of course raised another issue: how to walk back on our promise we were moving out without losing face? Especially since we'd walked out in such a dramatic fashion.

"We can always tell her that Charlene didn't want us," Dooley suggested.

"One phone call to Charlene would prove that to be a lie," I explained.

"Or... we could say that Harriet and Brutus begged us not to leave?"

"They would never corroborate our story, especially since we were supposed to leave together."

"So... what do we say, Max? Without looking silly?"

I sighed. "I think we'll have to bite the bullet and tell her the truth."

"What is the truth?"

"That we're very unhappy about this whole Boggle situation, but that we feel that we can't leave our human to face this situation all by herself."

And we would have walked back in, our story ready to go, when another stretch limo suddenly drew up at the curb, another blacked-out window rolled down, and this time it was none other than Opal whose famous face appeared. She, too, was wearing a pair of oversized sunglasses as she directed her attention at us. "Hey, you guys over there. Yes, you. Is this where Odelia Poole lives?"

"Odelia Kingsley," I said. "And yes, she does live here."

"Max, it's Opal!" Dooley loud-whispered.

"I know!" I whispered back.

"I have no idea what you're saying," Opal complained. But then she opened the car door and a small ginger cat hopped out. It was Prunella, Opal's sweetheart.

"Hey, fellas!" she cried, clearly happy to meet us again. We'd met Opal and Prunella in LA, when the family had flown out there to assist Opal with the small matter of someone trying to get her killed. We even stayed at her house that time.

"Oh, hey, Prunella," I said.

"Okay, I think this must be the place," said Opal, and also stepped out of the car and then up to the front door. When she rang the bell, this time Chase appeared. The big guy seemed momentarily stunned to find the well-known talk-show hostess on the welcome mat, but then a sunny smile creased his face.

"Opal Harvey as I live and breathe," he said. "So nice to see you again."

"Same," said Opal curtly, then glanced beyond him. "Is Odelia in? I need to have a word."

"Absolutely," said Chase, and disappeared indoors with this latest guest.

The door closed, and Prunella lamented, "She forgot about me! Can you believe that? She totally forgot about me!"

"It's fine, Prunella," said Dooley. "It happens to us all the time. Isn't that right, Max?"

"Especially lately," I muttered. "And I have a feeling it's only going to get worse."

CHAPTER 23

I have to say that the place was rocking: the Boggles were there, of course, John and Janine, with Tessa and Dante now added to the mix and also Opal Harvey. And right in the middle of it all was Odelia, looking a little over-wrought. Chase was by her side, darting an occasional anxious glance in his wife's direction, presumably worried that she might collapse under the strain.

"So I was thinking that this is the perfect time to sit you down for an exclusive interview, John," Opal was saying. "Especially with all that's been going on across the pond, this might give you an opportunity to put the record straight as far as your legacy is concerned."

"My legacy," John murmured approvingly, degusting the words with relish.

"You're pretty famous over here, too, you know, and people want to hear your side of the story."

"Absolutely, absolutely."

"It will give you a chance to tell the world about your body of work."

"Yes, yes, I would like that," said John, folding his hands

on top of his own sizable frame. "I would like that very much."

"And it will kick-start your new career," Tessa pointed out.

This had John look up in surprise. "New career? What's wrong with my old career?"

"Darling, that part of our life is over," said Janine gently. "You have to start thinking about the next chapter."

"You'll move to the States, of course," said Tessa. "Plenty of opportunities."

"You could launch yourself on the speaking circuit," said Opal. "If you play your cards right you could be a multimillionaire in a few short years. People pay plenty of money to listen to a man with your experience. A world leader. An icon. A legend."

"Leader, icon, legend," John murmured as his eyes twinkled excitedly.

"See?" said Janine. "What did I tell you? Instead of hanging on to that silly job of yours running that silly country and taking crap from a bunch of ungrateful people we should be following the money and living life in the lap of luxury."

Tessa nodded. "I'm talking Netflix deals, Spotify deals, exclusive podcasts, documentaries, speeches… Think billionaire, John, not millionaire."

"Yes, think big, bigger, biggest, John," said Janine.

"Big John," muttered John. "Bigger John. Biggest John."

"BJ," said Prince Dante. "That could be your brand, John. Team BJ."

"I don't think so, honey," said Tessa curtly. "Let's keep it strictly PG."

The Prince looked confused. "PG? I don't…"

"Let's hold a strategy meeting right here, right now," said Opal. She turned to Odelia. "Can we all stay the night? I don't want anyone to know about this meeting. This is all strictly hush-hush."

"Oh, Odelia would love to host us," said Tessa. "Isn't that right, Odelia?"

"I—" Odelia began to say, but the conversation had already moved on.

"You and Dante can take the main bedroom," Janine suggested. "And Opal can stay next door with Odelia's lovely folks. They've got plenty of space. Now let's get down to business. How soon can you get the ball rolling on that inter-view, Opal?"

And as the 'strategy meeting' progressed, without any input from Odelia or Chase, they both sort of melted into the background, presumably to announce to Marge and Tex that they were hosting the world's most famous talk-show host for the next couple of days, while the bright future of Big John was being discussed.

"I wonder where the dogs are," said Dooley, glancing around.

"Outside, probably," I said. "People like the Boggles or even Opal mostly keep dogs for show—as an accouterment or fashion statement."

"Dogs are fashionable?" asked Dooley, surprised.

"Oh, absolutely. And just like your regular fashion, what type of dog you should get changes every season. It might be Pekes this year and Chihuahuas the next. Though the type of dog you can carry in your handbag is the most convenient, of course. You can take them to New York Fashion Week or show them off on the red carpet at a movie premiere and be the talk of the town."

"Odd," said Dooley. "I've never looked at dogs as fashion objects before."

We decided to venture outside, to try and locate Harriet and Brutus, and tell them that the big move to Charlene was off. Now more than ever Odelia needed us, that much was obvious. Especially now that our home was under siege by all these millionaires—or was it billionaires—and was turning into a new Davos.

But when we arrived outside, of our friends there was no trace. We did come upon the first meeting between the Boggle dogs and Opal's precious little Prunella. One of those fateful meetings Netflix documentaries are made of.

"It's so great to finally meet you!" Little Janine was saying. "I'm your biggest fan!"

"That's nice," said Prunella coolly. "Who are you, exactly?"

"Little Janine," said Janine. "I told you. And this is Little John."

"Have we met before?" asked Prunella.

"Well... we met just now," said Little Janine uncertainly.

"We did? How strange. You'd think I'd remember." She then turned to us. "Oh, hey, Max and Dooley. So nice to see you again. Max and Dooley are some of my best friends," she told Little Janine. "They're the absolute best."

"Uh-huh," said Little Janine, ignoring me and Dooley. "There's so many things I want to ask you, Prunella. Like, is it true that you have your own chauffeur?"

Prunella stared at the little doggie. "I'm sorry, but who are you again?"

Dooley and I shared a grin. Prunella had played this game with us before.

She gave us a knowing wink, and we returned the wink with interest, even as Little Janine and Little John stood looking at each other with confusion written all over their faces. I could tell they hadn't expected their idol to also be a fruitcake.

"Let's get out of here, you guys," said Prunella, and headed in the direction of the opening in the hedge. "And where are Harriet and Brutus? Or don't they live here anymore?"

"Oh, they definitely still live here," I said.

"Though maybe not for much longer," Dooley added.

"Oh? And why is that? Tell me all, you guys. I've missed our conversations. And our adventures, of course!"

And so we told her all, even as we went in search of our friends.

CHAPTER 24

"*D*id you fly here on your private jet, Prunella?" asked Dooley as we traversed Marge and Tex's backyard.

"Of course. It's the only way to travel."

"If I had a private jet," I mused, "I wouldn't mind traveling the world and having lots and lots of new adventures."

"If I had a private jet," said Dooley, "I'd stock if full of kibble so Odelia would never run out again."

"You don't need a private jet to stock kibble, Dooley," I said. "You could stock it anywhere. In the basement, for instance, where it's kept nice and fresh."

This gave my friend pause. "If I had a private jet," Prunella began, then laughed. "How silly. I have a private jet, and I do travel the world all the time."

"I've always liked to stay home and stick close to my couch," I said, "but ever since our home turned into some kind of hotel, I'm starting to think that going places has its advantages as well."

"So why don't you? Go places, I mean," said Prunella.

"Oh, I don't know. Probably because Odelia is a small-town reporter, and so we like to stick close to our small town so she can write about our small-town adventures?"

"You have to think bigger, Max," Prunella enjoined. "Think global!"

"Global," I muttered. "But the world seems so... big."

"It is big, but also fun. Now where are Harriet and Brutus?"

"Is that Prunella's voice I'm hearing?" suddenly someone said somewhere in our vicinity. And when I looked closer I saw that Harriet and Brutus were hiding on the other side of the hedge.

"Are you playing hide and seek?" said Prunella good-naturedly. "Cause if you are, you've lost this round."

"Hey, Prunella," said Brutus as he emerged from his hiding place and shook a stray leaf from his person. "We thought we'd hide from Odelia's guests and this place is as good as any."

"You mean those two mutts? But they're harmless."

"Harmless but very annoying," I said.

"They treat us like surfers," Dooley added sadly.

"Yeah, they think the sun shines from their behind," said Harriet, causing Dooley to give her a puzzled look.

"How can the sun shine from their behind?" he asked. "That's impossible."

"It's just an expression," I said. "It means they think the sun rises and sets on them."

"But the sun does rise and set on them, doesn't it? And on us, too."

"Of course it does, Dooley, but they seem to think the sun revolves around them."

This gave my friend plenty of food for thought, for he was quiet for the next couple of minutes as he worked this out.

"Our home isn't our home anymore," Harriet lamented.

"The Boggles have taken over and they're driving us all crazy."

"Odelia first and foremost," I said. "Which is why we need to reconsider our plan to move in with Charlene, you guys. Odelia needs us now more than ever."

"I guess she does," Harriet agreed. "Though she brought this on herself. She should never have agreed when Tessa asked her to host those awful Boggles."

"Odelia is a nice person," I said. "She doesn't like to say no to her friends."

"So why don't you try and get rid of the Boggles?" Prunella suggested.

"Easier said than done," I said.

"Yeah, I have the impression they're here to stay," said Brutus.

"Look, Opal once had a guest I couldn't stand," said Prunella, "so I simply made his life miserable and in the end he left. It took some scheming on my part, and Opal wasn't happy with me for a while, but you know what they say: the end justifies the means." She shrugged. "So I simply did what I had to do."

We all fixed her with a curious look. "So what did you do?" asked Harriet.

Prunella smiled. "If I tell you, will you take me to your cat choir tonight? Ever since you told me about that I've been dying to join your choir."

"Of course," said Harriet. "You can even sing first soprano if you like."

I frowned at our friend. This was big. Harriet would fight anyone to the death if they dared to try and take away that particular privilege. It just goes to show how fed up she was with the Boggles.

"Well, the secret is—"

But what the secret of getting rid of unwanted guests

really was would have to remain a secret for a little while longer, for at that exact moment Tex joined us in the backyard, dressed once more in his coveralls, hard hat and high-vis vest. This time he was also donning safety goggles and looked ready to jump on board Jeff Bezos's or Elon Musk's or Richard Branson's spaceship and take a trip into space.

"Neighbor, oh neighbor," a voice sounded from the other side of the hedge.

"Ted," said Tex unhappily.

"About my gnome. I don't know if you've noticed, but someone demolished the pride of my collection." And to show Tex that he wasn't kidding, he held up what was left of a pretty large garden gnome. "See? Big Papa's head is gone. Pulverized."

"Have you considered that his head might have simply collapsed, Ted?"

"Collapsed? What are you talking about?"

"Plaster fatigue, Ted. I'm talking about plaster fatigue."

Ted stared at his neighbor. "You're pulling my leg, aren't you?"

"Absolutely not. Plaster fatigue is real, Ted. One moment you have a healthy, fine-looking gnome, and the next—poof! He's gone. Collapsed into a pile of dust."

For a moment, Ted was speechless as he stared from Tex to the remnants of his gnome. "Plaster fatigue," he murmured. "How about that?"

"Or it could be plaster rot, of course. The two conditions are equally fatal for your garden-variety gnome."

"But I bought it from a reputable seller, Tex. A very reputable seller."

"Don't believe everything you read online, Ted. There's a lot of frauds out there. Frauds and thieves. They'll prey on innocent collectors like us."

"Is that a fact?"

"Absolutely. So next time before you buy a gnome online, come to me first."

"I will do that, Tex. I will definitely do that. Thank you. Thank you so much."

"You're welcome, neighbor. Us gnome collectors have to help each other."

"That's... very kind of you."

"It's a gnome-eat-gnome world out there."

"Plaster fatigue," Ted murmured as he went on his way. "Well, I'll be damned."

And as Tex turned, a smirk on his face, he encountered the gaze of his mother-in-law, who stood wagging her finger. "You naughty, naughty boy, Tex Poole."

Tex's grin widened. "Takes one to know one, Vesta."

Gran, too, was dressed in blue coveralls, a high-vis vest, hard hat and safety goggles. And much to our surprise, they started clearing away the rubble that had once been the garden house. Not the fact that they were clearing the site was surprising, but the fact that they were collaborating and not at daggers drawn.

I guess miracles do happen, even in Bumpkin Cove.

CHAPTER 25

⤬

The moon rose radiant and serene on a peaceful world below. Hampton Cove was silent and not a creature stirred… or did it? Five cats slowly made their way to the park, where we were met by a striking scene: dozens more cats, all chattering excitedly and enjoying this meeting of the minds as they hung out at the playground. No happy kiddies gliding down the slide or clambering up the jungle gym now, but the collected cat population of our small coastal town.

"This is just… magical," said Prunella in hushed tones as she witnessed the amazing scene. "And you guys do this every night?"

"Every night," I said.

"At least when we're in town," said Harriet airily. "Like yourself we have so many international obligations that sometimes it's hard to find the time, but we feel it's impor-tant to give back to the local community, which is why we keep coming back as often as we can."

Prunella gave Harriet a sideways glance, then gave me a

knowing wink. "So who is Shanille and why is it important I talk to her?"

"Because she's in charge of cat choir," I said. "She's our director."

"A role she's still getting accustomed to," said Harriet. "But I have to admit that she's gradually improving—with a lot of assistance from her first soprano, of course." She tapped her chest self-importantly and threw her head back. "*Moi.*"

This time Prunella had to laugh, then quickly suppressed her mirth when Harriet gave her a scathing look. Of course when it comes to dealing with divas Prunella had probably seen it all, since half the divas of the world had at one time or another taken place in front of her human.

"And there she is now," said Harriet. She waved a deft paw. "Shanille, oh, Shanille. We have a guest tonight. And she's going to sing the soprano part."

Shanille, who's Father Reilly's cat, came walking over. As always she looked grave. Shanille takes her role very seriously. She gave Prunella the once-over. "You have to audition first, of course," she said, tapping her chin as she circled Prunella and studied her from every angle. "Is this your first experience as a singer? Because let me tell you, little missy, it's not as easy as it looks."

"I make it look easy," said Harriet with satisfaction.

"Many are called but precious few are chosen," Shanille clarified.

"Prunella is Opa—" I began to say, but Shanille cut me off with a gesture.

"Silence! This is no trivial matter, Max. This is cat choir, and we have standards—standards I adhere to very rigidly." She narrowed her eyes as Prunella's lips twisted into a smile. "Well, let's hear it," she snapped.

"What do you want me to sing?" asked Prunella.

Shanille shared a look with Harriet and said, "Why don't you sing Harriet's part for tonight? Hello."

"Hello to you, too," said Prunella with a grin.

"Don't get smart with me, young lady. I meant the song *Hello* by Adele."

"Not Adele!" said Prunella in mock shock.

"Only the best can join my choir," said Shanille. "The best of the best."

"In other words, the very best," said Prunella, then sighed. "Okay, so I guess I'll give it a shot. Don't judge me too harshly, though, Miss Shanille. I know I still have a lot to learn."

"Go on, then," said Shanille, slightly mollified. "We're all here to learn. The important thing is to try and be open to honest criticism. And be willing to work hard and improve." She closed her eyes. "Just give me your best shot."

Prunella took a deep breath, and launched into the well-known song. And even as she hit those first few notes, we knew we were in the presence of greatness. Harriet's jaw dropped, Shanille's eyes flew open, and Dooley and I shared a look of surprise. Even Brutus, who'd been straining at the proverbial leash to join his friends and shoot the breeze, stopped twitching. And when Opal's sweetheart got to the chorus, and belted out those high notes as if she'd never done anything else her entire life, we were all stunned. All around us, conversations halted, and soon all eyes were fixed on Prunella.

And when finally the song was at an end and the last notes drifted off into the night, for a moment you could hear a pin drop, then all of cat choir burst loose into a raucous applause and loud cheers.

"Amazing!" Shanille gasped. "I've never heard anything like it! You're a natural, Priscilla."

"Prunella," said Prunella.

"Yeah, that was pretty good," Harriet admitted, and nodded in admiration. High praise, coming from her.

"I've been singing all my life," said Prunella modestly. "It's one of my hobbies."

"Who are you?" asked Shanille.

"Prunella is Opal Harvey's cat," I explained. "She's in town for a visit."

"Opal's cat!" Shanille cried, and now looked as if she was about to collapse. "Why didn't you say so?"

"I tried," I said.

Shanille now placed a paw around Prunella's shoulder. "Let me introduce you to the others. And how is Opal as a human? Is she as nice in real life as she is on television?" And as she led Prunella away, the latter mouthed, 'Thanks, Max!'

"You're welcome," I said. Prunella might be rich and her owner famous, but from what I remembered she didn't have much of a social life out there in LA. It would do her some good to chat with other cats for a change.

"That was so amazing, you guys," Harriet gushed, now that both Prunella and Shanille were out of earshot.

"It was," I said. "It really was."

"I wish I could sing like that."

"You have to practice, Harriet," said Dooley. "The important thing is to try and be open to honest criticism. And be willing to work hard and improve."

"Wiseass," said Harriet good-naturedly, and sashayed off, ever the diva.

"See you around, fellas," said Brutus happily, and also pranced off.

And as Dooley and I mingled with our friends, suddenly I saw two familiar figures standing at the edge of the clearing, watching on with marked interest.

Reading from left to right, they were: Little John and Little Janine!

CHAPTER 26

*S*omehow I wasn't surprised to see the Boggle canines giving us the evil eye. Presumably they'd followed us all the way to the park, having nothing better to do than to play surveillance. It is, after all, what dogs do best: track down stuff. When it's not a bone they once buried in the backyard, it's their landlady's cats.

"It's the Boggle dogs, Max!" said Dooley, much perturbed. "They're watching us!"

"And gossiping about us, no doubt," I said.

"What are we going to do!"

"Just ignore them," was my advice.

"But how can we ignore them? They're right there—watching! Waiting!"

He was right. It's very hard to ignore a pair of dogs who are doing their utmost not to be ignored. They were so very obviously conspicuous I could see their game. They were trying to intimidate us. Browbeat us into submitting to them. But instead of allowing myself to be cowed, I decided to beat them at their own game. "Let's go," I said curtly.

"Go where?"

"Go and talk to them."

"Talk to them! But, Max!"

"Settle this thing once and for all."

And without waiting for Dooley's reply, I stalked over there, planting myself in front of the twosome and giving them the evil eye.

"Hey, Max," said Little Janine. "Fancy meeting you here."

"Let's cut the crap," I said, having had quite enough of this twosome.

"What a voice Opal's cat has, right?" said Little John, and suddenly I noticed that from up close the mocking expression I thought I'd detected on his face was actually more akin to admiration. "I've always been such an admirer, you know."

"Me, too," said Little Janine. "Remember how we used to watch her on the stage? I always thought she had it in her to be a star. And look at her now."

"She's the absolute best," Little John gushed. "She should have her own show."

"Wait, you knew that Prunella had such a great voice?" I asked, taken aback by this demonstration of abject fangirling —or as in Little John's case fanboying.

"Oh, sure," said Little Janine. "She once sang a song on Opal's show."

"It was magical," said Little John with a little sigh. "Absolutely amazing."

"We saw you guys head out and so we decided to tag along," said Little Janine. She gave me a bashful look. "We just figured you wouldn't want to be seen with us so we kept our distance."

"Cats like you don't like dogs like us," Little John explained.

"What do you mean, 'dogs like us?'" I asked. I was experiencing that sudden jolt you get when you walk down the stairs and think you've reached the ground floor only to discover there's one extra step you didn't count on. Very annoying!

"Well, obviously you're famous, Max, and so is the rest of your crew."

"Famous? What are you talking about?"

Little Janine laughed uncertainly. "Well… you're Max. *The* Max."

I stared at her, quite discombobulated. "Yes?"

"We've been reading about you, Max—in the *Gazette*. The articles Odelia writes? You're the cat she often refers to, aren't you? The Max from the stories?"

"But… do you get the *Gazette* over in England?"

"Of course we do, silly," said Little Janine. "The internet is everywhere."

I sank down on my haunches, shaking my head. I still didn't get it.

"Look, before Janine met John, she was already thinking of moving to Hampton Cove. You see, her grandparents retired here and so as a kid she spent her holidays here. And she always had this idea that she wanted to return one day and buy the house her grandparents had lived in and fix it up. But then of course life happened and she more or less put that idea on the back-burner, as one does. But then she met John and turns out he, too, once spent a summer here and fell in love with the place. They even think that they may have met that summer when they were both little, which makes Hampton Cove extra meaningful. Anyway, when John's political troubles began, Janine started thinking that maybe he should drop politics and start life afresh. With her. Out here."

"And so Janine has been a fan of the *Hampton Cove Gazette* for years," Little John continued the story. "It's been her life-line to this place—her favorite place."

"Which is why we were so excited to meet you guys. You and Dooley and Odelia and Chase."

"And Harriet and Brutus," Little John said with a smile.

Dooley, who'd finally screwed up his courage and had joined us, had caught the final part of the narrative, and he now piped up, "But you've been very rude to us. And you've treated us like those people in Downer Abbey. Those surfers."

"Serfs," I corrected him.

"That's what I said. Surfers."

"I know and I'm sorry about that," said Little Janine, giving us a look of quiet contrition. "It's just that…"

"Have you ever met one of your heroes in the flesh?" asked Little John.

I thought about this for a moment, then shook my head. "Actually, no."

"Max is my hero," said Dooley. "And I meet him every day."

"Oh, Dooley," I muttered, my cheeks coloring beneath my fur.

Little Janine smiled. "Well, you two are my heroes, and so when I met you I felt so… well, bashful I guess, and behaved in a very bad way. And I want to apologize."

"Me, too," said Little John. "We behaved shamefully. Absolutely rotten."

"I still don't get it," I said.

"Which is unusual for you, isn't it, Max?" said Little Janine, batting her eyelashes at me, causing me to feel even more as if the world had suddenly tilted on its axis and was giving me a kick in the tushy. "Usually you're pretty astute."

"Max has a big brain," Dooley said. "His brain is the biggest of all the brains of all the cats I know. Brutus says it's because he has a big head, but I don't think so."

"Okay, so the thing is that Janine wants to move to

Hampton Cove with John, only John doesn't know it yet," Little Janine explained.

"He isn't ready yet to let go of his political career," said Little John.

"Even though it looks as if his political career is ready to let go of him."

"So Janine and Tessa, who've known each other a long time, decided to work a scheme whereby they got John to agree to come here—just for a short sojourn. A way to decompress, and to get away from Westminster for a little while."

"Who is this Wes Minster? Is he John's dad?" asked Dooley.

"Westminster. It's the political heart of London," said Little Janine.

"And not a fun place to be right now for John," said Little John.

"No, they don't like him there very much at the moment."

"And so Tessa and Janine conspired to get John out here, and while he's here, they hope to convince him to chuck his career altogether and build a new life with Janine on this side of the Atlantic. Renovate her grandparents' place and settle down."

"Maybe even start a family," said Little Janine softly.

"They could have a baby," Dooley suggested. "Just like Odelia. I'll bet she can give them tips on how to go about it."

"I think John and Janine know how to make a baby, Dooley," said Little Janine laughingly.

"They do? Then maybe they can explain how it works, because it's still not completely clear to me," said Dooley, which caused our two guests to laugh heartily, much to Dooley's surprise. "What did I say?" he asked me.

"Nothing, Dooley," I said. "They're big fans of you, that's all."

"Big fans of me?" my friend asked. "How odd."

Little Janine now gave me a strange look. "Max?"

"Mh?"

"Do you think we could join cat choir? It's just that I've read so much about it and Odelia describes it so nicely in her columns."

Both Dooley and I stared at her. "Odelia writes about us?" I asked once I'd recovered from the shock.

"Of course she does, silly. Didn't you know?"

We both shook our heads slowly. "I never read the *Gazette*," I confessed.

"We know how the sausage is made," Dooley added. "And like every butcher knows, once you know how the sausage is made, you don't want to eat it."

This had Little John and Little Janine in stitches, causing Dooley to give me a helpless look. I merely shrugged. Apparently Dooley's fame as a standup comedian extended all the way to England. Who knew!

As it was, I didn't think it was a good idea to introduce two dogs into cat choir. So instead I took them over to a different section of the park, where dog choir rehearses, and introduced them to Fifi, Rufus, Lil Ran, Windex and the other members of dog choir. They were all very happy to welcome two new applicants, and before long the Boggle dogs were singing along to their little hearts' content.

And as Dooley and I made our way back to the playground, my friend said, "You see, Max? Never judge a cookie by its cover."

"I think you're referring to a book, Dooley."

"Pretty sure it's a cookie. Cookies have covers."

"So have books."

"Yes, but you can't eat a book."

Now how can you argue with that?

And he was right, of course. We'd gravely misjudged

Little John and Little Janine. So maybe Big John and Janine weren't as bad as we thought either?

Only time would tell. At least for now we might have to call off Operation Get Rid of the Annoying Guests. Since they might not be so annoying after all.

CHAPTER 27

⊱⊰

That night no less than five pets slept on the couch downstairs: Dooley and I, Prunella, but also Little John and Little Janine. I guess the couch was big enough for all of us. Harriet and Brutus slept next door, as usual, and I have to say that for the first time in quite a while I slept like a log. And even when Grace started screaming the house down in the middle of the night, it only registered as a blip on my radar. Maybe I was finally getting used to the presence of that little one?

Next to us, Wilkins slept on a mattress, presumably with his eyes open, like any personal protection officer worth his salt—keeping a keen look out for any potential intruders, political hitmen or annoying paparazzi.

Tessa and Prince Dante had opted to spend the night next door, sleeping in Marge and Tex's bed while the couple bunked with Gran on a spare mattress. And of course Opal had been granted the privilege of Odelia and Chase's bed, while the couple had also enjoyed the comfort of a spare mattress and slept on the floor.

What did wake me up was when Opal arrived downstairs

and started rummaging around, moving furniture and muttering to herself.

"What is she doing?" I finally asked Prunella.

"Setting up for the interview, of course," said Opal's sweetie.

"What interview?" I asked. "What are you talking about?"

"The interview with John Boggle."

"She's going to film that here? In our house?"

"And why not? Opal likes to film all of her interviews in other people's places. Though usually she likes to do it outside, with some scenic backdrop of some gorgeous greenery. Guess she doesn't think your backyard is fit for purpose."

"She could use the backyard next door," Dooley suggested. "It has a barbecue."

Prunella didn't look particularly impressed by this suggestion, but then not everybody likes a barbecue. Besides, ever since Tex had started work on his bathroom, his backyard was a mess. Not exactly the scene for an Opal interview.

"I hope we can be in the interview, too," said Little Janine.

"Oh, yes!" said Little John. "I've always wanted to be in an Opal interview!"

"We could lie at John's feet," Little Janine suggested. "And look solemn."

"I can do solemn. I can do solemn with the best of them!" said Little John.

"Why is Opal interviewing Big John?" asked Dooley. "Is he famous or something?"

"Opal likes to interview people who are in trouble and are ready to repent," I explained. "She interviews singers who've been bad, actors who are on drugs, athletes who've cheated, and pop stars who've been kept prisoners by their dads."

"So what category is Big John in? Has he cheated or is he on drugs?"

"I think he's done a bit of everything," said Little Janine vaguely.

Just then, the pet flap flapped and Harriet and Brutus walked in, both looking well rested and well groomed.

"How are things over here?" asked Harriet as she displayed a slight grin.

"Fine and dandy, I trust?" said Brutus, displaying the same type of grin.

I gave them both a look of suspicion. I wondered what they were up to.

"Fine," said Prunella with a yawn. "Everything just A-okay. Though I could do with a pedicure," she said as she regarded her left paw with a frown of concern.

"We have a pet salon in town," Dooley announced. "We can tell Odelia to make you an appointment."

Prunella gave him a sweet smile. "Thanks, Dooley. Are they any good?"

"I don't know," Dooley admitted. "Odelia never takes us there." Then his face lit up. "But she's taken us to the vet many times. Though we hate to go. She always prods us in the belly and pokes us with all kinds of needles."

Prunella grinned. "Just the kind of thing I like to hear on an empty stomach."

"You're welcome," said Dooley innocently.

Harriet and Brutus shared a look. "Seems to take a long time," Brutus remarked.

"I would have thought they'd have seen it by now," said Harriet.

Suddenly a terrifying scream tore through the house, startling us all.

"That's Janine!" Little Janine cried.

Wilkins, who'd been practicing his thousand-yard stare through the front window, immediately sprang to life. Like the man of action that he was, he was off and running in seconds flat. And of course cats being the curious creatures that we are, we were right behind him.

Wilkins got there first, of course, but we only trailed him by milliseconds—if you didn't know, cats are fast, if they choose to be. The sight that met our eyes was a horrifying one: straight out of a scary movie, in fact. Big John was there, just having woken up, his shaggy blond hair even shaggier than usual, with next to him Janine, who looked absolutely perfect, except for the expression of sheer disgust on her face.

Opal had also hurried up the stairs, and was now standing in the room, along with Odelia and Chase, providing their guests with an appropriate audience.

And there, smack dab in the middle of Janine's pillow, it lay: a perfectly wrought piece of poo.

"How ghastly!" said Opal, and darted an anxious look at Prunella.

"How inappropriate!" said Big John, and frowned at Little John.

"How nice and round," said Dooley, and gave me a look of admiration.

"Hey, it wasn't me," I said.

"Me, neither," said Prunella.

"And it wasn't me!" said Little John.

"Or me," said Little Janine, admiring the specimen.

"It stinks!" Janine cried in dismay. "The smell woke me up!"

"Oh, dear," Odelia muttered.

And of course, since nothing ever gets past her, Grace chose that moment to start wailing, drowning out all other sound.

"Who put that there!" Big John demanded, raising his voice over the hubbub.

Odelia had hurried off to see what was troubling Grace,

so Chase was left to make the assumptions. He walked up to the offending piece of poo and bent over it to take a sniff. "It smells like poo," he finally decided.

"You can tell he's a detective," said Dooley happily.

"Of *course* it smells like poo!" cried Janine. "It *is* poo! What I want to know is who put it on my pillow!" Her eyes suddenly widened. "Oh, yuck! I probably slept in it! John! Is it in my hair! Please tell me it's not in my hair!"

John subjected his wife's hair to a closer scrutiny and finally shook his head. "It is *not* in your hair," he solemnly declared, like the true statesman that he was.

"Thank God. I can't do an Opal interview with poop hair."

"Better wash it," Opal suggested. "Just to make sure."

"I don't know why," said Harriet. "It's not as if smell transmits through the television. As long as she looks good it doesn't matter if she smells bad."

She was smirking, I saw, and so was Brutus.

"You did this, didn't you?" I said. "Either you or Brutus."

"Or why not both?" Brutus quipped, visibly satisfied with himself.

And sure enough, suddenly Janine started screaming again and pointing a finger at her husband. "Your hair!" she bellowed. "It's in your hair."

And as all those present transferred their attention to the —present or former, the jury was still out on that one— Prime Minister of England, we saw that a piece of poo dangled from his unruly mop, right in front of his nose. He studied it now, looking cross-eyed for a moment, then seemed to sag somewhat. "Oh, snap."

CHAPTER 28

$\mathcal{T}$he unusual demarche of Brutus and Harriet was cause for a heated discussion outside, amongst our momentarily extended pet family.

"Why would you poop on my human's pillow?!" Little Janine demanded.

"And let's not forget about my human!" said Little John.

"Your human is my human and vice versa, John," said Little Janine.

"Oh, right, of course," said Little John. "So why would you poop on our humans' pillows!" he rectified his earlier statement.

Harriet looked taken aback by this sudden attack. Then she extended a paw in my direction. "Because Max told us to!"

I did a double-take. "What? I did no such thing!"

"Yes, you did. You told us to find a way to get rid of the Boggles. And so we devised a plan to get rid of the Boggles."

Little Janine and Little Janine now turned their ire on me. "I'm disappointed in you, Max," said Little Janine.

"I'm also disappointed in you, Max," said Little John.

"But I didn't say anything about pooping on our guests' pillows!"

"It was me," said Prunella, now stepping to the fore. "I told them to do it."

The two dogs' eyes went wide. "You!" Little Janine cried. "But why?!"

"Yes, why is what I'm also wondering," Little John chimed in.

"Because I could tell that Max and his friends weren't happy that you guys moved in. And so I told them how I once managed to get rid of one of Opal's unwanted guests by depositing a token of my lack of appreciation on his pillow. I got the idea from *The Godfather*," she explained. "But since I couldn't get hold of a horse's head on such short notice I decided to get creative and say it with poo."

Now Little Janine turned back to me. "You aren't happy that we're here?"

I regarded her a little shamefacedly. "I told you last night that you guys were being a little obnoxious, didn't I? Treating us like serfs."

"Yes, like the surfers from Downey Abbey," Dooley confirmed.

"All I wanted was to have our peace and quiet back."

"You can't imagine what we've had to endure," said Harriet. "First the baby arrived, causing us all to take a back-seat to the little one's wants and needs, and then you guys arrived and ate our food, took over our couch, used our litter boxes, spoiled our favorite rose bushes… It hasn't been a fun experience."

Little John and Little Janine had the decency to look contrite. "I know," said Little Janine. "And I've already apologized." Then she turned to her friend and housemate. "I told you not to eat everything and to leave some for the others."

Little John gave me a sad look. "Traveling makes me stressed, Max. And when I'm stressed I want to eat. So I ate. All of it and then some. I'm sorry, you guys."

"That's all right," I said. "I also like to eat when I'm stressed."

"And also when you're not stressed," said Brutus with a grin.

"So I can sympathize." I then glanced in Harriet and Brutus's direction, and gave them an encouraging nod. When they still didn't take the hint, I said, "And now Harriet and Brutus are also going to apologize for their appalling behavior." And since they still looked reluctant, I gave Harriet a prod in the rear.

"Ow! What are you—okay, all right, I apologize. I shouldn't have done what I did." Though I had the distinct impression she was secretly proud of her work.

"I also want to apologize," said Brutus with a big smirk. "I'm deeply, deeply sorry that I snuck into your humans' bedroom last night—which actually is our humans' bedroom —and left a message on their pillows. Though I can assure you it wasn't easy. Janine is a light sleeper. For a moment there I thought she was going to wake up and catch me in the act. So to speak."

"Yes, yes, yes," I said. "I'm sure Little John and Little Janine aren't interested to hear all the sordid details of your midnight marauding. And now I hope we can leave this entire episode behind us and move on."

Little Janine nodded. "I forgive you, Brutus, Harriet... and you, Prunella."

"Does your poo smell like roses, Prunella?" asked Dooley. "Cause you smell like roses."

"I wish!" said Prunella. "No, I'm sure my poo smells like your poo, Dooley."

"It does? So nice that we have something in common."

And so we decided to let bygones be bygones. And I have to say that once we'd moved past our differences, we all got along like sailors on shore leave. And when Fifi also joined us, and even Rufus decided to drop by, the gang was complete and a wonderful time was had by all. At least until we were shooed out of the backyard by Opal, who said we were obstructing the camera's view of the backyard, which she was going to use as the backdrop for the interview.

Once in Tex and Marge's backyard, we were met with a peaceful sight: Tessa and Dante were enjoying a delicious breakfast, accompanied by Tex, Marge and Gran.

"You have a lovely home here, Marge," said Tessa. "And a wonderful family."

"I know," said Marge, well pleased. "We're very lucky, my husband and I."

"And once we build that spa..." Gran began, but Marge shut her up with a single glance, and the old lady complied with an eye roll and a deep sigh.

"We were thinking of moving out here," said Tessa. "You have such a great quality of life here in Hampton Cove."

"Would be even better if we had a nice spa," Gran muttered.

"Is it true that Janine and John are thinking of moving here?" asked Marge.

Tessa and Dante shared a look. "I don't know," said Dante. "Where have you heard that?"

"Oh, I heard it from someone, can't remember who now. So is it true?"

"You'd have to ask them," said Dante diplomatically. He glanced down at me. "Hey, I remember this big guy now. He visited us back in London, didn't he?"

"I did," I confirmed. "So where is Fluffy? Didn't she come with you?"

"I seem to remember you had a dog?" said Marge, taking my hint.

"Oh, of course, Fluffy," said Tessa. "We left him in LA. The kids, too."

"Kids, plural?" I asked. My, my, they had been busy.

"Stop harassing the humans and let them enjoy their breakfast, Max," said Prunella, and so I stopped harassing the humans and we ventured further into the backyard.

I could have explained to Prunella that harassing humans is what we did, but Little John seemed to have picked up a scent, for he was gesticulating excitedly in the direction of the hedge. "I think I've got something!" he cried. "Must be a tabloid reporter!"

"John has been training Little John to sniff out tabloid reporters and paparazzi," Little Janine explained. "He dislikes them so much he's even told Little John to bite first and ask questions later, though I doubt Little John is capable of physical violence. He's more a peaceable kind of dog."

"It *is* a tabloid reporter!" Little John cried, wagging his tail. "I'm sure of it!"

"What's a tabloid reporter, Max?" asked Dooley.

"It's a reporter who works for a tabloid," said Harriet. "Isn't that obvious?"

Dooley chewed on this for a moment, then said, "What's a tabloid, Max?"

"It's a type of newspaper that focuses on the more sensational stories," I said.

"The more sensational the better," Little Janine explained. "Unfortunately they don't always distinguish between reality and fiction when they print their stuff."

Little John was barking up a storm now, jumping up against the hedge that divides our backyard from the next.

"That's not a tabloid reporter," said Rufus gruffly. "That's Ted. My human."

"Oh?" said Little John, a disappointed look on his little face. Then he rallied, like any good guard dog would. "Is your human Ted a tabloid reporter?"

"He's an accountant," I said.

This should have been the final blow to Little John's theory, but you can't keep a good dog down. "So maybe he's a tabloid reporter in his spare time?"

"No, he's not," Rufus snapped. "Now stop barking already, will you?"

"Oh, all right," Little John said, standing down.

"Oh, neighbor!" Ted said, his head now popping over the hedge.

Tex threw down his napkin and came over. "Ted?"

Ted was holding up his headless gnome again. "The thing is, neighbor, that you said Big Papa's head collapsed from plaster fatigue, remember?"

"I do remember, yes," Tex confirmed.

Ted tapped his face with a thoughtful finger. "Now I was wondering… if my gnomes are suffering from plaster fatigue, why was only Big Papa affected? Why didn't the heads of all my other gnomes turn to powder, too?"

"Well now, Ted," said Tex, bending over the hedge, "I'm afraid I can't give you an answer on that. You see, what you need is a gnome doctor, and I'm only a regular doctor."

Ted gave Tex a look of suspicion. "A gnome doctor?"

"You know, like a tree doctor?"

"I've heard of a tree doctor, but I've never heard of a gnome doctor before."

"Oh, they're rare and highly sought after. But I can assure you they exist. One of my gnomes once suffered from a rare fungus. I was afraid it was mildew or wilt so I contacted a gnome doctor and he said it was, in fact, diplodia tip blight and gave me a fungicide and it cleared up within a couple of days."

Ted moved his head back and forth in wonder. "Cleared it right up, huh?"

"It did indeed, Ted. Worked like a charm."

"Can you give me the name of this wonder doctor, Tex?"

"I'm afraid he passed away. But if I were you—and I want you to remember I'm not a tree doctor, all right?"

"Of course, of course."

"I'd get myself one of those powerful fungicides from the garden center and rub that stuff all over your gnomes. Really soak them in the stuff. It's the only way to make sure they won't suffer the same fate as the one you're holding there."

A sunny smile suddenly creased Ted's face. "Why, thank you, Tex."

"Don't mention it, Ted. One of the perks of having a doctor as a neighbor."

And as Ted went about his business, and so did Tex, Little John gave me a hopeful look. "Are you sure he's not secretly a tabloid reporter, Max? Cause he sure looks like one and he definitely smells like one."

"Will you stop with the tabloid stuff already?" said Little Janine. "Now for the most important question of the day. When and where is breakfast being served!"

It was a very important matter indeed, and so we all traipsed up to Marge, and I said, "Have you by any chance managed to replenish the kibble coffers, Marge?"

Marge smiled at this, and made the universal 'come hither' sign by crooking her index finger. We followed her into the house, and lo and behold: no less than seven bowls stood awaiting us in the kitchen, all laden to the brim with delicious kibble, one for each pet.

"And there's plenty more where this came from," Marge announced as we all happily dug in. And when I lifted an upturned face to thank her, my eyes gleaming and glistening with honest gratitude, she added, "Don't thank me. Thank

Opal. She's the one who decided to splurge. She felt you all deserved a treat."

"I love Opal," said Harriet.

"Now that's my human for you," said Prunella proudly.

CHAPTER 29

ood is important, but since we didn't want to miss Opal's interview with Big John, we made sure not to linger so we had a front-row seat for the historic sit-down between the famous talk-show host and the politician and his wife.

By the time we returned to the house, the living room had been modified to Opal's specifications, and lots of lamps had been placed just so, bathing the place in light. John looked less nervous than Janine, but then of course he probably has plenty of media experience.

Janine had dressed to impress, with a black dress and a gorgeous diamond pendant. Her blond tresses cascaded to her shoulders like a waterfall of gold.

"How do I look?" Janine inquired. "How is my hair? Do I have something between my teeth? Is my lipstick all right? Is it smeared across my teeth?"

"You look fine, my darling," said Big John. "You look absolutely smashing." He gave her a comforting pat on the knee, then adjusted his tie, which was a bright yellow number with little red bells. Very stylish. Or at least very noticeable.

The audience had been requested to remain absolutely quiet, and consisted of the entire Poole family, and also Tessa and Dante, who watched the proceedings with interest. It isn't every day that you're present when greatness is in the making.

"Okay, when you're ready..." Opal prompted. She had donned a purple dress with a silver brooch and looked perhaps even more smashing than Janine, if that was even possible.

"Ready," John said, giving Opal a goofy grin and two thumbs up.

"When is she going to interview Odelia?" Dooley whispered.

"I don't think she's going to interview Odelia," I said. "This is all about John and Janine Boggle."

"But we're in Odelia's home. She should at least do the introductions."

"It doesn't work like that, Dooley."

"Oh." He lapsed into silence while Opal set the scene to the viewers at home.

"So maybe Harriet could sing a song during the intermission?" Dooley piped up again. "Or Prunella. She's such a great singer, isn't she, Max?"

"She is, but now if you could please be quiet? I'd like to listen to the interview."

"So, John, can you reveal something about your future plans?" Opal was saying. "A little birdie told me something about a possible Netflix deal? And a Spotify deal for a new podcast? And of course a big book deal? Is that true?"

John seemed to waver for a moment, then clasped Janine's hand in his and said, "As you know, I've thought long and hard about this, Opal. And even though the things you suggest all sound very intriguing and very interesting indeed... I don't think they are where my heart lies. If I'm absolutely honest with myself, what I want, what I really, really want... is to spend some quality time with my wife. These last couple of years have been pretty brutal on her—I think she's spent more time with our dogs than with me. And now that I've decided to take a step back from the political arena, the next few years of my life are hers."

Janine uttered a surprised gasp as Big John turned to her.

"Janine, I know you've been wanting to buy a house in Hampton Cove and start a family. Well, I want that, too. I want to have kids with you and I want to buy the house that your grandparents built and turn it into a home for us and the kids. At least," he added, a touch of hesitance in his voice, "if that's all right with you?"

"Oh, John," said Janine, and promptly broke into a flood of tears.

"Why is she sad, Max?" asked Dooley. "I thought she wanted kids?"

"Those are tears of happiness, Dooley," I said. "She's so happy she's crying."

"Huh," said Dooley, and I could tell he found this all very confusing indeed.

"So how about the Netflix deal, John?" Opal insisted. "And the book deal? And the Spotify deal?"

But John made a slicing gesture with his hand. "They're all off the table, Opal. I'm not doing it."

"Are you sure, John?"

"Yes, Opal. I want to be a dad. And a good husband. Nothing more than that." And suddenly he, too, burst into a flood of tears. "Darn it! Now you made me cry!"

"Opal has that effect on people," Prunella confirmed. "It's her secret power."

And when I looked around me, I saw that everyone was sobbing, even Chase!

"Are they all happy, Max?" asked Dooley, observing the same phenomenon.

"I guess so," I said. It was disconcerting to see so many grown people cry, but we all know that humans are weird at the best of times. Hearing a man declare that he doesn't want to be a billionaire but a dad must have touched a chord.

Of all the people present, Tex was actually crying the most. Then again, he might have been imagining how many gnomes one can buy for a billion dollars.

The interview wasn't at an end, but Little John must have thought it was, for he suddenly started barking furiously, causing Opal to halt in mid-question.

"It's a tabloid reporter!" Little John cried. "This time I'm sure! I can smell it!"

We all looked over to the window where the little doggie was pointing, and sure enough, an individual was peering in through the window and holding up his phone, presumably snapping shots of all of us.

"It's Otis Robbins!" Tessa yelled. "He works for the *Daily Pail*!"

"I'll give him a good bollocking," Dante growled, getting up.

But before he could give him this bollocking, whatever a bollocking was, Little John and Little Janine were already on the case, hopping in the direction of the kitchen door, slipping out through the pet flap, and the next moment we were all treated to a scene of a tabloid reporter being accosted by two furious dogs!

"Get off!" the reporter was screaming. "Get off me!" But instead of heeding his call, the two dogs snapped at his heels and tried to get a bite out of his ankles. And so Mr. Robbins quickly skedaddled, and as we moved to the front of the house, we could all see through the window how the man was being chased down the street, Big John and Janine's dogs right on his tail!

"Good riddance," said Tessa. "I can't believe he followed us all the way here."

"I think he was following us," said Big John. "He's not a big fan of my work."

"Or mine," said Janine as she dabbed at her eyes. "My face is a mess, isn't it?"

"Your face is beautiful," said John as he gave her a tender kiss on the cheek. "And so are you."

"Did you really mean what you said? About buying my grandparents' house and starting a family?"

"Of course. There's nothing I want more."

"Can you please save it for the interview," asked Opal, clapping her hands. "Let's get back into position, folks. I'm not done with you yet!"

A crackling sound came from the baby monitor, and we all looked up. The next moment Grace's loud wailing sounded through the room and Chase quickly got up. "I'll go," he assured his wife.

"She probably needs a new diaper," said Odelia.

"Don't worry, I'll do it," said Chase, and was off at a trot.

"A glimpse into the future, John," Opal remarked. "This is going to be your life from now on."

John gulped, then promptly teared up again, and started blubbering like a baby.

"Look how happy he is," said Dooley. "He can't wait to start changing diapers!"

CHAPTER 30

"I wish there was an Opal for pets," said Little Janine with a sigh. "The things I would tell her…"

"I could be the Opal for pets," said Harriet. "I think I'd do a great job. And the camera obviously loves me."

"Don't we already have an Opal for pets?" asked Dooley, and gestured to Prunella.

Harriet gave Prunella a not-so-friendly look. "You have to have the ambition to become a world-famous talk-show host, of course, and I'm not sure Prunella has that ambition."

"Definitely not," was Prunella's response. "Though if Opal keeps cloning me I could have a very long career in show biz. An indefinite career, in fact."

Now there was a thought. Since the original Prunella had been cloned several times, and this particular Prunella was the sixteenth iteration of the original version, she probably had a point. And if pets could be cloned, why not famous talk-show hostesses?

"Opal should have herself cloned," I suggested. "She could keep doing what she's doing… in perpetuity!"

160

"Interesting suggestion," said Prunella. "Maybe you can talk to your people, and they can talk to my people."

The interview was finally in the can, and all those gathered seemed pleased as punch. Except for one person, who stood musing on the sidelines, and regarding Opal with a grave expression on his royal face.

"Prince Dante looks unhappy," said Brutus. "I wonder what's wrong with him."

We were about to find out, since he now approached Opal and whispered something in her ear. A moment later the two walked out into the backyard. And since curiosity is a cat's second name, we all followed, wondering what was up.

"The thing is, Opal," said Prince Dante, clearing his throat, "that all this talk about becoming a billionaire and signing lucrative deals left and right… Well, I'm not sure it's really my thing, you know."

Opal stood listening intently to the young royal. "What do you mean?" Then she held up her hands. "Oh, no. Don't tell me you want to move to Hampton Cove and live the quiet life, too!"

"Actually… I was thinking more along the lines of doing the exact opposite." He released a deep sigh. "I've been feeling so homesick I could cry, Opal."

"You want to move back to England."

He nodded furiously. "I miss my friends, I miss my family. I miss… polo matches and cricket games. LA is all fine and dandy, and the weather is a nice bonus, but… I even miss the rain, can you believe it? Rain and snow and smog!"

"Have you discussed this with Tessa?"

"No, I have not."

Opal planted both hands on her sizable hips. "Why not, pray tell?"

The prince shrugged. "I'm afraid that if I tell her she

won't like it. And besides, what's the point? She'll never want to leave home and return to my country."

"I wouldn't be too sure about that, sonny Jim," said Opal. She placed a hand on the young man's arm. "You want my advice?"

He nodded anxiously.

"Talk to your wife. Tell her how you feel. You can't keep this to yourself, Dante. This is an important discussion and if you keep bottling up those feelings they're going to form a barrier in your relationship. They're going to eat you up inside."

The young prince's bottom lip was quivering dangerously as he took this in.

"He's going to cry," said Brutus.

"No, he's not," said Harriet.

"I think he's going to laugh," said Dooley, who always has trouble reading human emotions. "See? He's going to burst into a big laugh any moment now."

But instead, the prince suddenly burst into a flood of tears, and as Opal gave him a big hug and patted his back consolingly, he was letting it all out.

"Oh, Opal, I just want to go hoooooooome!" he blubbered.

"There, there," said Opal. "Don't hold back."

And he certainly didn't.

The next moment Tessa came walking up, drawn by the wailing sounds, and so Opal transferred the teary prince to her care, walking away with an expression on her face that unmistakably said: 'I still got it, you guys!'

"Isn't this annoying for you?" I asked Prunella, "that wherever your human goes people spontaneously burst into tears?"

"Oh, you get used to it," said Prunella as we moved back into the house.

"I really thought he was going to laugh," said Dooley. "Humans are very hard to read, Max."

"I know, Dooley. They're a strange species."

Once inside, Marge also approached Opal for a brief one-on-one, and they removed themselves from the scene. But since I had a feeling she was going to use this opportunity to complain about Gran's bathroom habits, I decided not to follow. After all, there's only so many heartfelt tears a cat can stand in one day.

CHAPTER 31

"So what have we learned, Dooley?"

"That politicians have feelings, too, and that princes like rain?"

"And that when your brother-in-law is dating the mayor you shouldn't build illegal bathrooms in your backyard," I said. Especially when that mayor is a regular guest in that same backyard and can see firsthand what you're up to.

Charlene might be a good friend of the family, but that didn't mean she was prepared to turn a blind eye to shoddy building work constructed without the necessary permissions. And so as quickly as it began, Tex's DIY project came to an end. It had taken the united efforts of the good doctor, Chase and Alec to resurrect the garden house in its full splendor—more or less—and a strong-worded convo between Opal and Gran to get the latter to promise to be more considerate in the future when using her allotted bathroom time, to put an end to this episode.

I settled back on the porch swing, after having eaten my fill of the tender meat Odelia had placed before us, and sighed contentedly. It takes your home being overrun by guests to realize how perfect your life really is. Odelia had revealed to us that she wasn't actually planning to turn her house into an Airbnb—or a home in the sky, as Dooley referred to it—and the guests who had come, had now gone.

"They could at least have stayed for the barbecue," said Dooley as he began licking his paws.

"I think Tex's reputation as a grill master precedes him," I said. "And since no one likes to run the risk of being poisoned, they decided it's better to be safe than sorry."

"At least we'll still see them, since John and Janine are moving to Hampton Cove." He glanced around. "Where are Harriet and Brutus, by the way?"

"In the rose bushes." Ever since Odelia had discovered that our canine visitors had turned her backyard into a dog lavatory, she'd removed the last vestiges of Little John and Little Janine's sanitary deposits, much to our eternal gratitude.

John and Janine had found a place to stay in town, and had started negotiations to buy back the house Janine's grandparents built. And as Dooley had indicated, Little John and Little Janine had become a fixture at dog choir.

"You could always build a composting toilet, Tex," Charlene now suggested.

The humans were all gathered around the family table, while Tex provided them with nuggets of delicious food, straight from the grill (with the kind but insistent assistance of his son-in-law and brother-in-law).

"Don't you need permission to build a composting toilet?" asked Gran.

"Well, no, actually. And it's a lot easier to install than outdoor plumbing."

"You can always use our bathroom, Dad," said Odelia. "Just pop in any time."

"Thanks, honey," said Tex, looking slightly embarrassed

to be discussing his bathroom needs with the rest of the family.

"Or you could buy yourself an RV and park it out here," Scarlett suggested.

Charlene grimaced. "I'm afraid you can't use an RV as an annex to your home, Scarlett. It has to permanently retain its means of mobility to leave its location at any time."

"Holy fudge," said Scarlett. "Did you learn the entire municipal code by heart?"

"As a matter of fact I had another citizen come in last week who wanted to do the exact same thing: install an RV in his backyard. So I had my administration look it up. Which is why I can tell you that I strongly advise against the idea, Tex."

"My suggestion is to knock down that back wall and do your business in Blake's field," said Gran. "Nothing like an early-morning tinkle in nature."

Tex's cheeks colored. "Okay, so we have sausages, burgers, delicious ribs…"

"I have the impression he doesn't like to talk about his bathroom habits, Max," said Dooley.

"Who does? It's a very private part of our existence, Dooley. Not something to discuss over dinner."

"I don't mind. I can discuss my bathroom habits all day long. For instance, this morning I noticed Odelia has switched litter. The new kind has this weird smell."

"It's called baby powder," I said. "And it's supposed to be very popular."

Dooley's jaw fell. "Baby powder! But, Max! Why do babies have to die so our litter can smell nice?!"

"What are you talking about?" I said, as I eyed a piece of sausage coming my way as carried by Marge, who kindly deposited it between my front paws.

"Powderized babies, Max. We've been doing our business on dead babies!"

"Baby powder is made from talc, Dooley, which is a mineral. No babies are harmed in the making of the stuff. Now eat your sausage."

"Yes, Max."

And for the next few moments only the sounds of chewing could be heard, as we masticated our meaty treat. But you can't keep a chatty cat quiet, and Dooley said, "I'm glad it's just us again, Max. It's fun to have guests, but it's even more fun to watch them leave."

Which is the slogan of Airbnb if I'm not mistaken. But he was right, of course. I was glad to have the place to ourselves again. Opal and Prunella had returned to LA in their private jet and I'm sure Opal had gone right back to reducing celebrities to tears with her in-depth interviews. Tessa and Prince Dante had a long talk about their future, and decided to get a second home in London and fly back and forth more regularly from now on. And maybe hold off on the ambition of world domination for the time being. And John and Janine had moved into the Star Hotel for now, while negotiations were underway to acquire the house her grandparents built and turn it into their new family home away from home.

But of course that's not what you are interested in, is it? The question that is burning on your lips right now is whether Ted Trapper finally found a cure for the plaster fatigue his gnomes are suffering from. And I'm happy to say that the answer to that question is an emphatic yes and a four-chair turn. Ever since Ted started rubbing his gnomes with a powerful fungicide, no more gnomes have lost their heads, which makes Tex's gnome-loving neighbor a very happy man indeed.

"So... Max?"

"Mh?"

"Is it true that cats are more intelligent than dogs?"

I frowned at my friend. "Where did that come from?"

"Oh, just something Gran said the other day. She said dogs come from wolves, while cats come from lions and tigers. And everyone knows that lions are a lot cleverer than wolves and when it came to a showdown lions would win paws down because lions are the king of the jungle and wolves aren't." He'd said all that without taking a single breath of air, which amazed me. "So that means that we are king of Hampton Cove and we can eat dogs for breakfast, right? Right, Max?"

From over on the Trapper side of the hedge, Rufus had joined us, and from over on Kurt's side, Fifi now came tripping up and hopped up onto the porch.

"What's going on, you guys?" said Fifi happily. "Mh, sausage," she added when Chase walked by and dropped a piece of sausage in her lap.

"I love sausage," said Rufus in his deep voice and gave Chase a look of absolute devotion when the latter extended him the same sausage-dispensing courtesy.

When he saw that we were suddenly cornered by dogs, Dooley gulped a little. "Okay, so let's just say that when it comes to a showdown between a cat and a dog, it might be a draw. But only just," he quickly added.

"What is he talking about?" asked Rufus.

"Dooley thinks cats are smarter than dogs," said Fifi.

"I didn't think you heard," Dooley muttered as he shrank a little.

"I may not be as clever as you, Dooley, but there's nothing wrong with my ears, thank you very much. Mh, this is some good stuff. Tex is definitely improving."

"I'm sorry, Fifi," said Dooley. "I just want to say that I consider you an honorary cat. You, too, Rufus."

Rufus frowned. "What does that even mean?"

"It means that I don't think of you as a dog but as a cat. Well, almost. You're not a real cat, of course… Not like me, I mean. You're like… a wannabe cat?"

Both Rufus and Fifi were exchanging amused glances.

"What I mean is…" He blinked, discovering he'd talked himself into a corner.

"I think you better stop talking now, Dooley," I suggested.

"No, but I mean—what I actually mean is…" Finally he gave up. "I have no idea what I mean. I just want to say is that I like you, Rufus, and I like you, Fifi, and it doesn't matter if you're a cat or a dog, I consider you both my best friends."

"Aww," said Fifi, and gave Dooley a nudge. "That's sweet of you to say, Dooley."

"Yeah, very considerate," said Rufus. "For a cat you're okay, Dooley."

"Not as okay as a dog, obviously," said Fifi. "But you're not so bad."

At Dooley's look of confusion, they both laughed. And when Dooley finally realized they were pulling his paw, he smiled and said, "Oh, you guys!"

We might make fun of dogs in these chronicles of mine from time to time, but at the end of the day I think dogs are just swell. But please don't tell them I said that. They just might grow too big for their britches—or their collars.

THE END

Thanks for reading! If you want to know when a new Nic Saint book comes out, sign up for Nic's mailing list: nicsaint.com/news

EXCERPT FROM BETWEEN A GHOST AND A SPOOKY PLACE (GHOSTS OF LONDON 1)

Chapter One

"I didn't think you'd show up," the gruff voice announced.

Harry looked up from her perusal of the latest James Patterson. She quickly closed the book and shoved it into her backpack, then rose from her perch on the low wall of the underpass. She shrugged as she approached the hulking figure. "I'm always true to my word," she told the man, doing her best not to look or sound intimidated.

He really was a giant of a man, though she'd been told he wasn't as dangerous as he looked. He could have fooled her, though. He had no neck to speak of, his arms alone were probably as thick as her waist, and she could have fitted several times in the long black overcoat he was wearing, she herself being rather on the petite side.

She pushed her blond tresses from her brow and fixed her golden eyes on the stranger, rubbing her hands to keep warm. She'd removed her gloves and knitted cap and now thought perhaps she shouldn't have. The cold drizzle that had started overnight had turned into a real downpour, and even though they were protected from the brunt of the autumn weather by the underpass, the wet cold still crept in Harry's clothes and chilled her to the bone.

"Let's do this," the man grumbled. "I haven't got all day."

The watery sun that had tried to pierce the dark deck of clouds that afternoon had finally given up its struggle, giving free rein to the driving rain. But then this was London, a city that for some reason had collectively decided the sun had no business here, except on those very rare occasions.

She quickly unzipped the main compartment of her backpack and took out the package, then handed it to the client. Through the clear plastic protective cover it was easy to make out its contents, but the burly man insisted on taking the book out nonetheless.

"You're going to get it all smudged," Harry murmured, though she knew this was none of her business. Once the transaction was made, the book belonged to the client, to do with as they pleased, whether she liked it or not.

"Looking good," the man muttered, flipping through the pages of the voluminous tome. "How do I know it's the real deal?"

"You have Sir Buckley's word," she said with a light shrug.

The client scrutinized her carefully, shoving the book back into its plastic covering. Then he nodded once. "Good enough for me," he announced. He handed her a small black briefcase. "One million. As agreed," he told her.

She balanced the briefcase on her knee and clicked it open. Two thousand 500 pound notes should be there and as far as she could determine they were all present and accounted for. But then again, she didn't think the client was going to cheat her. And even if he did, Buckley would handle it.

So she clasped the briefcase under her arm and looked up at the man, a little trepidatious. Buckley had always told her to conclude the meeting the moment the transfer was done, and only rarely did a client linger. This one still stood staring at her, however, as if their business wasn't concluded yet. They were the only two people there, as the underpass was quite deserted.

This was Buckley's favorite place to make a transfer, as this particular spot wasn't covered by any of London's half a million cameras. Which also meant that if a client decided to get any funny ideas, Harry had no recourse. It wasn't as if she had a black belt in jujitsu or some other martial arts discipline. She'd recently watched a video on the Daily Mail website on how to protect yourself against an attack, but hadn't the foggiest notion how to execute those nifty self-defense moves in real life.

The man gave her an unexpected grin, displaying two gold teeth. It was something you didn't see that often these days, and she found herself staring at the shiny snappers before she could stop herself. Along with his bald dome, it gave him the aspect of an old-fashioned James Bond bad guy. But then his smile suddenly disappeared, and he gave her a curt nod. "I guess that concludes our business," he grunted.

"Yeah, I guess it does," she returned.

He abruptly flipped his hoodie over his head, then turned and walked away. Soon he was swallowed up by the shadows stretching long tendrils of darkness beneath the overpass. Moments later she heard a motorcycle kicking into gear, and then its roar as it raced away into the falling dusk.

She heaved a sigh of relief. These exchanges were going to be the death of her one day, she thought as she hurried out of the underpass, to where she'd fastened her bicycle to a streetlight. Fortunately, it was still where she'd left it. She tried to fit the entire suitcase into her backpack but failed, so she tipped its precious contents into her trusty Jack Wolfskin rucksack and dumped the suitcase in a nearby trashcan. And as she adjusted the straps, she noted a little giddily she'd never worn a million pounds on her back before. Then she pressed her pink knitted cap to her head, used her gloves to wipe that fabled London precipitation from her saddle, mounted the bike and was off.

Five minutes later she was pedaling down Newport Street, anxious to get back to the store. She'd only feel at ease once the money was safely transferred to Sir Geoffrey Buckley's cash register. And as she waited for the traffic light to turn green, she idly wondered what she would do with so much money. She could quit her job, buy herself a great house and take that trip around the world she'd been dreaming of for ages. The lights changed, and traffic was off and so was she, stomping down on her silly daydreams. The money wasn't hers and never would be. She was, after all, only a lowly wage slave in Sir Buckley's employ. Why there was a Sir in front of his name, she didn't know, even after working for the man for close to a year now.

Buckley Antiques, the store where she spent her days when her employer wasn't sending her to dark and creepy places to exchange packages with obscure and dangerous-looking clients, was a smallish shop tucked away in the more dingy part of Notting Hill. It carried rare antiques and other items for the connoisseur, its owner and proprietor, the eponymous Sir Geoffrey, priding himself in his capacity to obtain items for his clients that no other antiquarian could find. There was a whiff of the illegal and the criminal attached to both the man and the shop, and oftentimes Harry wondered where he obtained these rare and exclusive items if not by illicit means.

She'd never asked, and Buckley had never told her, of course. She merely did as she was told, and delivered million pound books to men with no necks without asking pesky questions. Such as: why would anyone buy a book for such an incredible price? And why not transfer the items at the store? She didn't ask because she was afraid she wouldn't particularly like the answer.

She couldn't help wonder, though, where the priceless tome would end up, for No-Neck, like Harry herself, was probably only the messenger.

But even though Harry knew that her employer was something of a high-end fence, her conscience was no match for her need of a regular paycheck.

With her history degree she didn't stand much of a chance to find a decent-paying job in London, or anywhere else in the United Kingdom for that matter, and she knew she should be grateful to have found a job at all that was a cut above being a waitress, cleaning lady or nanny. The job might not be completely on the up and up, but it was better than being on welfare.

Besides, for her discretion Buckley paid her a nice little stipend around the holidays, so there was that as well.

She attached her bike to the lantern in front of the store, and entered the shop, her trusty backpack burning with the money. As she stepped inside, the doorbell jangled merrily. As usual, the store was dimly lit, Buckley's way of adding atmosphere. She picked her way past the antique cupboards and Louis XIV armoires and tried to ignore the quite horrendous oil paintings adorning the walls. When she reached the counter, fully expecting to find Buckley pottering about, she was surprised to see him absent from the scene.

No sound could be heard, either, except for the ticking of a dozen antique Swiss cuckoo clocks Buckley had obtained from a Swiss traveling cuckoo clock salesman. A real bargain, he'd called them, though Harry failed to understand who'd ever want to pay good money for such monstrosities.

"Buckley?" she called out. "Buckley, I'm back!"

Usually the prospect of money brought out her employer like the genie from the bottle, but no frizzy-haired elderly gentleman popped up now.

Harry shrugged, and started transferring the money from her backpack to the cash register, which had a deep and convenient space beneath the money drawer. Here it would be quite safe until Buckley put it in the ancient but very sturdy vault he kept in his office.

She wondered briefly if she shouldn't close up the shop, as she wasn't even supposed to be working today. Buckley had called her in to deal with this urgent delivery, and she'd grudgingly complied. He didn't like to deal with his 'special clients' himself, reserving that particular privilege for her.

And it was as she stood wondering what to do when she became aware of a soft groaning sound coming from deeper into the shop. It seemed to come from the back. With a slight swing in her step, relieved to be rid of the huge pile of money, she decided to take a look. She didn't like to lock the door without Buckley's say-so. He had this thing about wanting the store to be open at all hours, even if that meant she had to take her lunch break in between serving customers. But she didn't like to leave it unattended either.

She would just have a look around and as soon as she'd found her employer—probably messing about somewhere in his office—she'd go home. After riding around in the rain for the past half hour she was wet, tired and numb, and a hot shower and some dry clothes looked pretty good right now.

Besides, she needed to put in some shopping and wanted to get it done before rush hour, hoping to salvage what little she could from her day off.

"Buckley?" she called out as she moved deeper into the store. Behind the showroom were two smaller rooms. One was Buckley's office, where he liked to meet with clients and suppliers, and the other was the small kitchen reserved for personnel—which meant her. It wasn't much. Just a table, some chairs, a sink, gas stove and fridge. Next to the kitchen a staircase led upstairs, to the apartment Buckley rented out for a stipend. In exchange, the man, who was rarely in during the day, kept an eye on the store after six.

"Buckley?" she tried again. She noticed that the door to his office was ajar, so she pushed it open. And that's when she saw her employer. He was stretched out on the floor, his limbs arranged in an awkward pose, blood pooling around his head. She clasped a hand to her face, her throat closed on a silent scream, and looked down at the lifeless body. It was obvious she was too late. His eyes were open and staring into space, his face pale as a sheet.

"Oh, Buckley, Buckley," she finally whispered hoarsely, automatically taking her phone from her pocket with quaking hand and dialing 999.

Minutes later, the store was abuzz with police and medics, as she sat nursing a cup of tea in the kitchen, stunned and fighting waves of nausea.

She looked up when she became aware of being watched, and she saw a man looking down at her from the entrance to the kitchen. He was tall and broad and easily filled the door-frame, both in width and height. She noted to her surprise that he was gazing at her with a scowl on his handsome face. Perfectly coiffed dark hair, steely gray eyes, chiseled features and an anvil jaw lent him classic good looks, and for a moment she thought none other than David Gandy himself had wandered into the store, mistaking it for the scene of his latest swimwear shoot. But then the man cleared his throat.

"Inspector Watley. Can I ask you a few questions, Miss McCabre?"

She nodded, wiping a tear from her eye. "Yes, of course, Inspector."

The inspector took a seat at the table and placed a small

notebook in front of him, checking it briefly. "Your name is Henrietta McCabre?"

"Yes, but most people just call me Harry," she said softly.

"You were the one who found the body, Miss McCabre?"

"Yes, I did," she said, tears once again brimming in her eyes.

"And what time was this?"

"Must have been... around four. I'd just come back from an errand."

He gave her a dark look. "An errand connected to the store?"

She nodded again. She was loathe to reveal the nature of her errand. Even dead, she didn't want to betray Buckley's confidence.

"Tell me exactly what you saw," Inspector Watley said gruffly.

She quickly told him what had happened, and didn't forget to mention the groan she'd heard—the sound which had alerted her of Buckley's presence.

Watley's frown deepened. "You heard a groan, you say?"

"Yes, I did. It's the reason I came back here. I thought Mr. Buckley had stepped out of the store, as he didn't respond when I called out. So when I heard the groan, I went looking for him... And that's when I found him."

"That's odd," the inspector said, fixing her with an intent stare.

"What is?"

"The groan."

"Why odd? It is perfectly natural for someone who's just tumbled and knocked his head to groan. I'm just surprised I didn't hear it sooner."

"According to the preliminary findings of our coroner, Mr. Buckley must have been dead for at least half an hour before you arrived, Miss McCabre."

This news startled her. "He was dead... before I arrived?"

"Yes, he was."

"Oh, poor Mr. Buckley," she said. "To think he'd been lying there all this time before I found him! If only I'd arrived sooner, he could've been saved." She looked at the policeman. "I knew this would happen. I just knew it."

He stared at her blankly. "You knew he was going to die?"

She nodded. "He was very unsteady on his feet lately. Only last month he took quite a tumble when he stepped from the store. I told him he should get a cane, but he was far too proud." She shook her head, extremely distraught. "It was only a matter of time before he took a bad fall and hit his head."

The policeman eyed her curiously for a moment, then lowered his head and said slowly, "Your employer didn't hit his head, Miss McCabre."

"What do you mean? If he didn't hit his head, then how did he die?"

"Mr. Buckley was murdered, Miss McCabre. Murdered in cold blood with a blunt object by the looks of things." Then, without waiting a beat, he went on, "Can you account for your whereabouts between the hours of three and four, Miss McCabre?"

Her jaw dropped. Was he accusing her of murdering her own boss? "Well, I wasn't here if that's what you mean," she was quick to point out.

"Where were you then?"

And she was about to respond when she remembered she couldn't. Even though providing herself with an alibi was more important than respecting Mr. Buckley's wishes, she still couldn't tell the inspector where she'd been. Not if she didn't want to get in big trouble with No-Neck and his employer.

Chapter Two

It didn't take a genius to figure out she was in a pickle. Not only didn't she have an alibi, but apparently the safe was empty, all of Mr. Buckley's possessions stolen. It was obvious how things looked from Scotland Yard's point of view. They probably figured she'd burgled the safe, seeing as she knew the combination, was caught in the act by her employer, at which point a violent struggle had ensued and she'd violently slain the older man. The only reason she wasn't being placed under arrest was that she'd be an idiot to stick around after the murder, or to call the police herself.

These and other thoughts were now swirling in Harry's head as Inspector Watley told her tersely to please remain available for questioning—probably the Scotland Yard equivalent for 'Don't leave town!'

She nodded quickly, her face now completely devoid of color and her extremities of blood, and wobbly got to her feet the minute Watley left.

And as she made her way out of the store, which was still swarming with police, she feebly wondered what she was going to do now. For one thing, she was most definitely out of a job. Which was something she should have told Watley, she now saw. Clearly she had no motive for murder; it simply meant unemployment. Then again, she'd just tucked a million pounds of motive into the shop till, and who knew how much more money Buckley kept in his safe, along with countless other valuables? Plenty of motive there.

As she rode her bicycle home, the rain was coming down again in sheets, and even before she'd reached the street where she lived, she was soaked to the skin. A fitting ending to a lousy day, she thought miserably.

Arriving home at Valentine Street No. 9, she quickly fastened her bike to the cellar window grille, wiped the rain from her eyes, and jogged up the steps to the front door. Letting herself in, she stood leaking rainwater on the black and white checkered floor for a moment, then slammed the heavy door shut, and quickly checked the mailbox. A magazine had arrived—the historical magazine she subscribed to —and a bill from the electric company, probably announcing another rate hike.

She hurried up the stairs, already shucking off her jacket, and when she arrived on the landing wasn't surprised to find her neighbor patiently awaiting her arrival, Harry's snowy white Persian in her arms.

"Oh, shoot," she said, taking the cat from the elderly lady. "Did Snuggles sneak into your flat again, Mrs. Peak? I thought I locked her up this time."

Mrs. Peak, the wizened old prune-faced lady who lived next door, gave her a wistful smile. "I don't mind, Harry. I only wish she visited me more often. I wouldn't mind having a darling like Snuggles myself, you know."

"Perhaps one day you will," said Harry as she pulled Snuggles's ear. "If she keeps this up, I just might have to give her away."

Mrs. Peak didn't seem to mind one bit. "Snuggles can drop by any time," she assured her.

"Thank you, Mrs. Peak," she said, letting herself into her flat. And as she closed the door, she whispered, "What's the matter with you, little one? Why do you keep sneaking off to the neighbors, huh? Don't you like it here?"

She put the cat down on the floor and looked around her modest flat. It wasn't even a flat, really, more of a studio apartment. One living room with kitchenette, a small bedroom, and an even smaller bathroom. Just enough for the student she'd been when she took it, and currently all she could afford on her meager earnings. She'd told herself back then that once she got her first paycheck she was going to find something bigger. But then she'd seen the paltry sum on her paycheck and had realized that it would be a long time before she'd be able to afford anything more than what she had. In fact she was lucky to have a place as nice as this one, London quickly becoming too costly for anyone without a millionaire mum or dad to foot the bill.

She watched as Snuggles haughtily stalked to the window, which was open to a crack, hopped out onto the small balcony, and started to make her way over to Mrs. Peak again. Harry quickly hurried after her and managed to snatch her just before she hopped from her balcony to the next.

"What's wrong with you?" she asked as she took the cat indoors again and closed the window. "Do you get special treats next door? Is that it?"

She checked Snuggles's bowl, but it was still filled to capacity. Possibly she was simply bored with the same dry food and needed something fresh?

And she was just scooping some canned food into a second bowl, much to Snuggles's delight, when she remembered she'd scheduled a call with her cousin.

She hurried over to her laptop, flipped it open and switched it on. And as she made herself a jam sandwich and carried it on a plate to the laptop, she kicked off her soggy sneakers, then hopped into the bedroom to change into something dry. She was just wrapping a towel around her head when the telltale sound of Skype warned her that Alice was online and calling her.

Video image of her cousin flickered to life, and she gave her a jolly wave.

"Hey, honey," Alice said. "Did you just step out of the shower?"

"No, I just stepped out of London, which is basically the same thing."

Alice laughed. She was a perky blonde with remarkable green eyes, and perennially in a good mood. "You should come and visit, Harry. It's about eighty degrees out here and not a single cloud in sight."

Harry sighed. "That sounds like heaven. I wish I could, but…"

"The antique shop, huh? Too much work? I can relate, honey. I'm actually holding down three jobs right now if you can believe it. The mortuary, the gun store, *and* the bakery. Never worked so hard in my life!" Harry nodded absently, and Alice's face fell. "Are you all right? You look very pale."

She shook her head. "Something horrible happened to me today, Alice."

She proceeded to tell her cousin about the murder of her boss, and Alice cried, "Oh, no! You must have been terrified! How are you holding up?"

"I'm… fine, actually. Though at the moment I seem to be the only suspect the police have." She tucked a leg beneath her and told Alice the whole story.

She and her cousin had no secrets from each other. They'd always been close, ever since Alice's father, Curtis Whitehouse, had been stationed in London, working at Scotland Yard in an advisory capacity for five years. Since Uncle Curtis and Aunt Demitria had lived right next door to Harry's parents, she and Alice had been like sisters. The bond had never been broken, even now, when they were thousands of miles apart.

"So they think you have something to do with the murder?"

"Judging from the look on Inspector Watley's face, yes. And I can't even give him an alibi, as my client would never forgive me."

"Who is he?"

She shrugged. "Probably some rich businessman who

doesn't want to pay full price for his works of art. Most of them are, Buckley once told me."

"Can't you ask? This No-Neck person must be traceable, right?"

"Actually I have no idea how to get in touch with him. Buckley always made all the arrangements. I just had to show up to make the exchange."

"If I were you I'd try to find the guy," Alice suggested. "Otherwise you're in big trouble, honey. The police will be very suspicious if you won't tell them where you were." She shook her head. "Oh, how I wish I could help you."

She didn't see how she could, though. Even though Alice's father was now chief of police in the small town where he and his family lived, he had no clout with Scotland Yard. Unless…

"Does your father still keep in touch with his old colleagues?"

"He might," Alice admitted. "Do you want me to ask him?"

"Could you? Perhaps if I can just talk to someone, I can explain what happened without betraying the client's confidence."

"All right. Sit tight, hon. I'll give him a call now." Then she paused, looking thoughtful. "You know? There's actually someone else who might be able to help you."

Harry took a bite from her sandwich. She suddenly found she was starving. "There is? Who?"

"He's, um…" Alice bit her lip. "He's a guy who knows people, you know."

"Yes?"

Alice stared at her for a beat. "I'll have to discuss it with him first, though."

"Okay," she said, a little puzzled. It wasn't like Alice to suddenly go all mysterious on her. "Is he from England?"

"No, he's American, but he might know someone over

there who can help you." She eyed her anxiously. "I worry about you. You're all alone out there."

"I'll be fine," she said, though she realized that she didn't sound very convincing. It was true that she was quite alone out here. Her parents had died in a car crash the day of her graduation, and since she didn't have any sisters or brothers she basically had to rely on herself. She had an aunt and uncle up in Scotland but hadn't heard from them in ages. The only family she kept in touch with was Alice, which was at least something to be thankful for.

Alice seemed to make up her mind. "I'm going to talk to Brian. I'm going to ask him to pull a few strings."

"Oh, okay," she said. "Who's Brian?"

Alice closed her lips, her face turning red. "I, um, didn't I mention him?"

"No, you didn't." She laughed. "What? Is he, like, your new boyfriend or something?"

"No, of course not! Reece and I are still very much together. You know that."

Alice was engaged to Reece Hudson, a famous movie star. Even Harry had seen a couple of his movies. He was a great guy and loved to goof around with Harry when he and Alice came to London. The couple usually stayed at the Ritz-Carlton, just about the swankiest place Harry had ever seen. Reece wasn't impressed, though. Said he'd stayed in far more luxurious hotels in other parts of the world. Which just went to show how the other half lived.

"Look, I've gotta go," Alice suddenly said.

All this talk about this mysterious Brian had apparently made her nervous, for she flinched when Harry protested, "You still haven't told me who this Brian guy is."

"I'll tell you all about him, honey. But first I need to get him to agree to something." She gave her a long look before asking her the most outrageous question of all. "Do you still... see things, Harry?"

She frowned. "See things? What do you mean? What things?"

"You know. When we were kids, sometimes you used to tell me you saw people who weren't really there, remember? Like... dead people?"

She laughed. "Come on, Alice. You know that was just my overactive imagination."

"No, but you said you saw Gran, remember? You even talked to her."

She did remember, though only vaguely. It was true that when her and Alice's grandmother had passed away, she'd imagined seeing her, after she had supposedly passed on. The old lady had visited ten-year-old Harry's bedroom the night she died. She'd told her that everything would be fine, and that she was moving on to a different plane but that she'd always watch over her and Alice. Later she'd begun to think she'd imagined the whole thing.

"You know that was just a dream," she told her cousin, but Alice didn't seem convinced. "I mean, what else could it have been, right?"

A slight smile played about her cousin's lips, but then she nodded. "Yeah, probably a dream. Anyway, I've got to go."

"Let me know what your father has to say, all right? I really hope he knows someone on this side I can talk to."

"Will do, honey. Love you! Bye-bye!"

She rang off and stared out the window for a while. The rain was lashing the single pane, and the sky was pitch black, even though it wasn't even fully evening yet. Snuggles jumped on her lap and installed herself there, purring contentedly. She stroked her behind the ears. "So it was the food, huh?" she murmured as she settled back.

She thought about what Alice had said about Brian, and

wondered what that was all about. But then she figured it had nothing to do with her, and decided not to expect too much. Alice had a habit of making a lot of promises before promptly forgetting all about them. And seeing as she was so busy, it would be a small miracle if she even remembered to ask her father about his Scotland Yard contacts. If he still had any left. It'd been almost ten years since he'd returned to the States and became Happy Bays's chief of police.

She thought back to Inspector Watley, and the dark looks he'd given her. It was obvious that if it were up to him, he'd have arrested her on the spot.

She heaved a deep sigh. "We're in deep trouble, Snuggles," she murmured. "If things don't look up it's not such a bad idea to head on over to Mrs. Peak for your kibble. She might just be your new owner from now on."

She shivered and moved over to the window to close the curtains. For the first time in a long time she didn't have anywhere to be the next day.

Chapter Three

Jarrett Zephyr-Thornton III was perfecting his ice skating technique when his personal valet beckoned him from the side of the rink. As per his instructions, the rink had been closed off to the public to allow Jarrett to practice in private. It was his dream to become the next big thing in figure skating, and since he'd never been on the skates before, but he'd seen all the movies, he knew that practice made perfect, so practice it was.

He was a spindly young man with wavy butter-colored hair and pale blue eyes that regarded the world with child-like wonder. As the son of the richest man in England he was in the unique position to do whatever he wanted whenever he wanted to do it, and what he wanted more than anything right now was to be the next British figure skating Olympic champion.

He groaned in annoyance when he caught sight of his valet Deshawn's urgent wave. "I told you to hold all my calls!" he cried, but the music pounding from the speakers drowned out his voice. It was the soundtrack of *Ice Princess*, of course, playing on a loop. Motivation was key, he knew, and he watched the movie at least once a day to keep him in the right frame of mind.

Reluctantly he finished his pirouette and swished over to the side.

"Yes, yes, yes," he grumbled when Deshawn handed him the phone. "This is Jarrett!" he called out pleasantly when it was finally pressed to his ear. "Oh, it's you, Father," he said with an exaggerated eye roll. "What am I doing?" He frowned at Deshawn, who shrugged. Father never asked him what he was doing. Just as Jarrett made it his aim in life to do as little as possible, his pater made it his habit to interfere as infrequently as possible, lest he develop a heart condition. "I'm ice skating, if you must know," he said a little huffily, fully expecting a barrage of criticism to be poured into his ear at this confession. "For what? The Olympic Games, of course. What else?"

"Look, son, something's come up," the author of his being now grated in his ear. "I need you to listen to me and listen to me very carefully, you hear?"

He did listen very carefully, even though he was quite sure that whatever the old man had to impart was probably a load of poppycock as usual. "Yes, Father. I am listening," he announced with another eye roll. There was a crackling noise on the other end, and then his father said, "I need you or that valet of yours to go over to..." There was that crackle again.

"There seems to be some sort of noise. What did you just say?"

"I need you to pick up the parcel and bring it to…"

"I'm losing you," he said, quickly losing patience.

"The parcel is at… right now, and if you don't pick it up… it's going to… along with your mother's… and that'll be the end of…"

"You're not making any sense," he said, staring down at his nice new blue spandex outfit. He'd bought seven, a different color for each day of the week. He particularly liked the one he was wearing now. It looked exactly like the one Michelle Trachtenberg, the star of *Ice Princess*, wore in the movie. "What package? And what does Mother have to do with anything?"

"Will you just listen!" the old man yelled, now audibly irritated. "If you don't pick up that package right now… then… and… unmitigated disaster!"

He sighed. Whatever his old man was involved in, it could probably wait, so he said, "First get decent reception, Father, and call me back, all right?"

And he deftly clicked off the phone and handed it back to Deshawn. He then gave his valet a look of warning. "No more phone calls, Deshawn."

Deshawn, a rather thickset smallish man with perfectly coiffed thinning brown hair and an obsequious manner, had been in Jarrett's employ for many years, and the two formed rather an odd couple. One thin and tall, the other short and stout, they resembled Laurel & Hardy in their heyday.

The valet now muttered, "I know, sir. My apologies. But your father said it was extremely urgent."

"It's always urgent," said Jarrett with an airy wave of the hand. "But he'll just have to wait, for I…" He glided away. "… am on my way to greatness!"

And with these words, he allowed the wonderful music of

Ice Princess to guide him back onto the rink and launch him into his most complicated movement yet: the twizzle, a one-foot turn. He usually worked with Vance Crowdell, trainer to the stars, but the man had some other arrangement tonight, so he'd been forced to train alone. Not that he minded. The crusty old trainer had already taught him so many new movements he needed to practice until he'd perfected those before learning any new ones.

And as he closed his eyes and allowed the music to take him into a new and wonderful world of glitter and glamor and thunderous applause, he saw himself as the first male Olympic figure skating gold medalist to come out of Britain in quite a long time.

❧

Philo eyed the woman darkly. "I'm not asking, Madame Wu. I'm telling you. Take the package and hand it over as soon as you're told."

"But I can't," the proprietress of Xing Ming lamented in nasal tones. Her jet-black hair clearly came from a bottle and her horn-rimmed glasses were too large for her narrow face. She'd been running the small family restaurant for thirty years, one of the mainstays of London's Chinatown in the City of Westminster. "I have other matters tonight. I can't do package right now."

He thrust the package back into her hands. "Just take it already. Lives depend on this," he added with a meaningful look. A look that said it was her own life that depended on it.

She rattled the package, her eyes unnaturally large behind the glasses. "What is it? Is it bomb?"

"No, is not bomb," he said, mimicking her accent. "It's just something very important." He leaned in. "Very important to Master Edwards."

A look of fear stole over her face, and she nodded quickly. "Yes, yes. Master Edwards. I will hand over package no problem. Hand over who?"

"You'll know her when you see her."

"Is woman?"

"Apparently."

Actually he didn't know himself. All he knew was that his contact had told him he would send his assistant, and she would be dressed in black. But since no one else knew about the package he wasn't too worried. He pointed a stubby finger at Madame Wu. "Just make sure she gets it, all right?"

She nodded, tucking the package beneath the counter. "Of course, Philo."

And as he stepped from the restaurant, the smell of Chinese food in his nostrils, he shook his head. Used to be that people like Madame Wu wouldn't dare contradict him, but that was before Master Edwards had fallen ill. The rumor that the old man was on the verge of death was spreading fast, and already his criminal empire was crumbling and his influence waning.

He crossed the busy street, bright neon lights announcing all manner of Asian food from every corner, and mounted the motorcycle he used to get around London in a hurry. And then he was off, narrowly missing the entry into the Chinese restaurant of a slender woman, all dressed in black.

It didn't take him long to race across town to his employer's house, in the heart of the East End. Master Edwards's house was located in a gated community, his own people providing protection, and Philo nodded to the guard as he passed. He'd hired him personally. A short drive up the hill led him to the house at the end of the street, which towered over all others. It used to belong to a famous actor in the sixties and was a sprawling mansion with fifty rooms, an underground pool, and cinema where Edwards and his cronies enjoyed watching gangster movies. Or rather, that's how it used to be.

He parked his bike in the garage and mounted the stairs, deftly making his way upstairs until he reached the landing and heard the telltale sounds of Master Edwards's snoring. Entering the bedroom, where the bedridden gang leader was laid up, he wasn't surprised to find him sound asleep. The moment he flicked on the light, the old man awoke with a start.

"Philo!" he muttered, blinking against the light. "Is that you?"

"It is, Master."

A look of annoyance crept into the man's eyes. "Why did you wake me?"

"Just to tell you that the package is being delivered as we speak."

The man's irritability dwindled. "Good," he said, settling back against the pillow. "Very good. Let's just hope the book works as advertised."

"I'm sure it will."

The old man licked his dry lips. "A lot depends on this, Philo. But then I probably don't need to remind you."

No, he didn't. He'd reminded him plenty of times since the chain of events had been set in motion a fortnight ago.

"There's only one small matter left to attend to," he said.

Master Edwards, whose eyes had drooped shut, opened them again. "Mh? What's that?"

"There's a witness," he said. "A young woman by the name of Henrietta McCabre. She's seen my face and might possibly become a nuisance."

"So?" snapped Master Edwards. "Just get it done, Philo. You don't need my permission to handle such a minor detail."

"No, Master," he said deferentially, though of course he did need the other's permission. In Master Edwards's world nothing ever happened without his approval, and most definitely not something of this importance.

"See to it that she's silenced, Philo. And make sure nobody sees you this time," the old man snapped, before closing his eyes once again. Soft snores soon sounded from the bed, and Philo bowed his head and retreated from the bedroom of his employer of twenty-five years. In this, the man's final days, he wasn't about to disappoint him. Not if he valued his own life. Henrietta McCabre, whoever she was, would not see her next birthday, he would make sure of that. And as he stalked over to his own room in the mansion, he sat down at the computer to begin an intense study of the life of Henrietta 'Harry' McCabre. This time, there would be no mistakes. And no witnesses.

ABOUT NIC

Nic has a background in political science and before being struck by the writing bug worked odd jobs around the world (including but not limited to massage therapist in Mexico, gardener in Italy, restaurant manager in India, and Berlitz teacher in Belgium).

When he's not writing he enjoys curling up with a good (comic) book, watching British crime dramas, French comedies or Nancy Meyers movies, sampling pastry (apple cake!), pasta and chocolate (preferably the dark variety), twisting himself into a pretzel doing morning yoga, going for a run, and spoiling his big red tomcat Tommy.

He lives with his wife (and aforementioned cat) in a small village smack dab in the middle of absolutely nowhere and is probably writing his next 'Mysteries of Max' book right now.

www.nicsaint.com

A Purrfect Gnomeful

Purrfect Cover

Purrfect Patsy

Purrfect Son

Purrfect Fool

Purrfect Fitness

Purrfect Setup

Purrfect Sidekick

Purrfect Deceit

Purrfect Ruse

Purrfect Swing

Purrfect Cruise

Purrfect Harmony

Purrfect Sparkle

Purrfect Cure

Purrfect Cheat

Purrfect Catch

Purrfect Design

Purrfect Life

Purrfect Thief

Purrfect Crust

Purrfect Bachelor

Purrfect Double

Purrfect Date

Purrfect Hit

Purrfect Baby

Purrfect Mess

The Mysteries of Max Box Sets

Box Set 1 (Books 1-3)

Box Set 2 (Books 4-6)

Box Set 3 (Books 7-9)

Box Set 4 (Books 10-12)

Box Set 5 (Books 13-15)

Box Set 6 (Books 16-18)

Box Set 7 (Books 19-21)

Box Set 8 (Books 22-24)

Box Set 9 (Books 25-27)

Box Set 10 (Books 28-30)

Box Set 11 (Books 31-33)

Box Set 12 (Books 34-36)

Box Set 13 (Books 37-39)

Box Set 14 (Books 40-42)

Box Set 15 (Books 43-45)

Box Set 16 (Books 46-48)

The Mysteries of Max Big Box Sets

Big Box Set 1 (Books 1-10)

Big Box Set 2 (Books 11-20)

The Mysteries of Max Shorts

Purrfect Santa (3 shorts in one)

Purrfectly Flealess

Purrfect Wedding

Nora Steel

Murder Retreat

The Kellys

Murder Motel

Death in Suburbia

Emily Stone

Murder at the Art Class

Washington & Jefferson

First Shot

Alice Whitehouse

Spooky Times

Spooky Trills

Spooky End

Spooky Spells

Ghosts of London

Between a Ghost and a Spooky Place

Public Ghost Number One

Ghost Save the Queen

Box Set 1 (Books 1-3)

A Tale of Two Harrys

Ghost of Girlband Past

Ghostlier Things

Charleneland

Deadly Ride

Final Ride

Neighborhood Witch Committee

Witchy Start

Witchy Worries

Witchy Wishes

Saffron Diffley

Crime and Retribution

Vice and Verdict

Felonies and Penalties (Saffron Diffley Short 1)

The B-Team

Once Upon a Spy

Tate-à-Tate

Enemy of the Tates

Ghosts vs. Spies

The Ghost Who Came in from the Cold

Witchy Fingers

Witchy Trouble

Witchy Hexations

Witchy Possessions

Witchy Riches

Box Set 1 (Books 1-4)

The Mysteries of Bell & Whitehouse

One Spoonful of Trouble

Two Scoops of Murder

Three Shots of Disaster

Box Set 1 (Books 1-3)

A Twist of Wraith

A Touch of Ghost

A Clash of Spooks

Printed in Great Britain
by Amazon